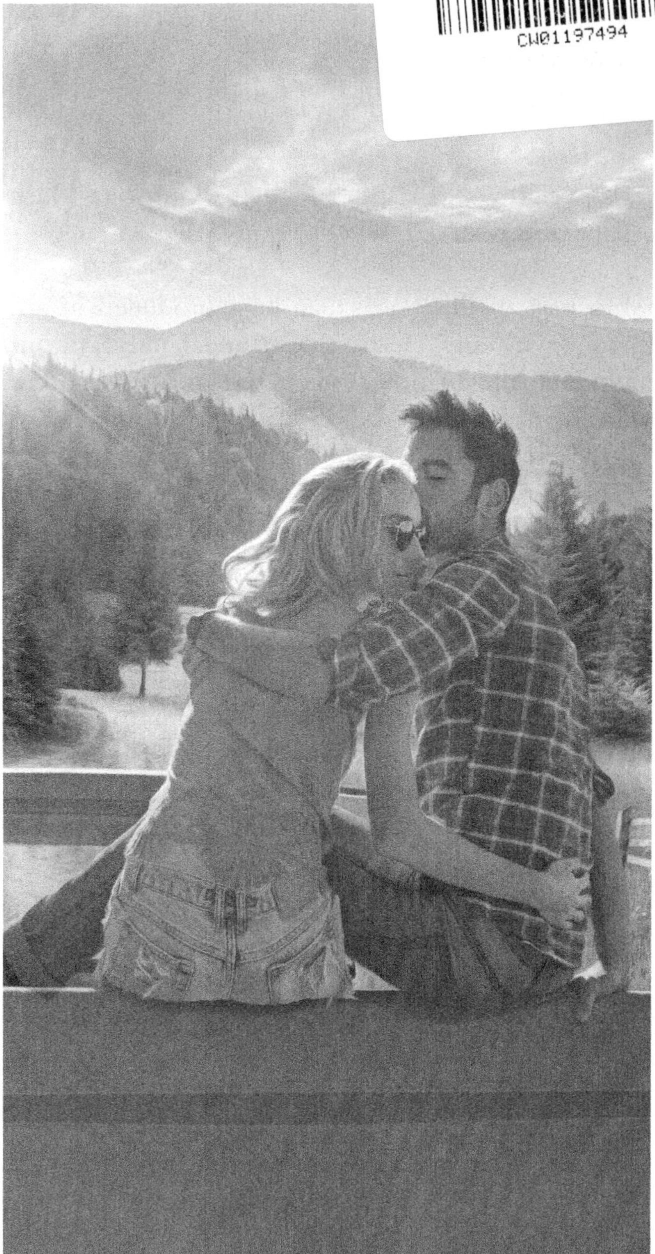

Copyright © 2025 by Jennie Marts
All rights reserved.

No part of this book may be reproduced in any form or by any electronic or mechanical means, including information storage and retrieval systems, without written permission from the author, except for the use of brief quotations in a book review.

This book is licensed for your personal enjoyment only. This book may not be re-sold or given away to other people.

AI RESTRICTION: The author expressly prohibits any entity from using this publication for purposes of training artificial intelligence (AI) technologies to generate text, including without limitation technologies that are capable of generating works in the same style or genre as this publication. The author reserves all rights to license uses of this work for generative AI training and development of machine learning language models.

This book is a work of fiction. Names, characters, places, and incidents are either a product of fiction or are used in a fictitious manner, including portrayal of historical figures and situations. Any resemblance to actual persons living or dead is entirely coincidental.

Cover Design & Interior Format:
The Killion Group, Inc.

LOST AND FOUND
Cowboy

LASSITER RANCH

JENNIE MARTS

*This one is for the misfits, the strays,
the fiercely loyal, and those
who choose their family through love…*

*And to those who are still searching…
may you find the place where you truly belong*

Chapter One

FAMILY MEANT EVERYTHING to Mack Lassiter, which is why he'd just driven fifteen hours to make it back to Colorado for his brother's wedding, but if he didn't get a move on, he was going to miss the whole thing.

It had been less than a year since he'd found out he had three half-brothers and a grandfather running a ranch in the mountains of Colorado, and it meant a lot that they'd included him in the wedding party. Which is why he'd driven all night and most of the day, pounding coffee and Reese's Peanut Butter Cups, to get back from the ranch he'd been working in Texas, determined to be there for Chevy's wedding. He'd only just found his brothers—he wasn't about to lose them.

Although he may have already lost the woman he'd also found in this small town of Woodland Hills, Colorado—the one who had filled his thoughts the past seven months he'd been toiling away in Texas. She'd stopped texting him—or maybe he had stopped texting her—days spent working a ranch are long and demanding and tended to blend together.

Fresh out of the shower, he scrubbed his hair dry with a towel then pulled on the new pair of jeans that had been left on the bed for him next to a black garment bag bearing his name. Being the new guy in town, and to this family, he was thankful he'd at least get to feel like himself in jeans and his own cowboy boots instead of dressed up in a fancy tux, which he'd never worn in his life.

His brother had told him the wedding would be held on their family's ranch and would be a more casual affair, but Mack was a little confused when he unzipped the garment bag, expecting to find a blue men's shirt with a silver vest and navy tie, and instead pulled out a small formal gray dress.

Hmmm. He glanced down at the garment bag again. The tag clearly read *Mack Lassiter.*

His brothers were famous for playing pranks on each other—and a small frisson of pride filled his chest to think they now considered him close enough to prank—but there was no way anyone expected him to wear this tiny dress.

It obviously wasn't meant for him.

Beyond the fact that the style of the light gray dress, with its high neckline and matching jacket, looked like something his former neighbor lady—who had to have been ninety, if she was a day—would wear to church, the thing was miniscule. There was no way it would fit any part of his well over six-foot frame.

The door of the bedroom flew open, and Lorna Williams, the single mom he'd been thinking about, and the sister of the bride, burst into the room. He wasn't sure if she'd taken her maiden name of Gibbs back, but Chevy had told him that her divorce from the no-good snake who'd run out on her while she'd been pregnant, had gone through while he was gone.

And it was no wonder he couldn't get this woman out of his mind.

She looked gorgeous in a silvery-blue dress that clung to her tall, curvy frame in all the right places. Her blonde hair was pulled up in some kind of fancy twist, but a few wisps had come loose and the sight of them resting softly against her bare neck sent his pulse racing like the lead car on the track at Daytona. He'd never seen her in high heels, and the strappy, silver sandals she had on made her legs look even longer.

"Ford, we've got a problem, and I need your help," she blurted, then froze as she must have realized that, although Mack was standing in his bedroom, he was *not* his oldest brother, Ford.

"Wow. I mean…hi." He shook his head and tried to clear his suddenly dry throat. "I mean, hey Lorna." He fumbled for the right words to say to the woman he'd thought about every day since he'd been gone. The same woman who'd deposited him firmly in the 'friend zone' before he'd left. "You look…stunning."

Still frozen, she stared at him, her eyes wide. Her mouth opened to speak, then closed again, then opened once more. "Mack," her voice came out in a whisper. "What are you doing here?"

His brow furrowed. Surely, she didn't think he'd miss seeing his brother get married. "I'm here for Chevy's wedding."

"I wasn't sure. I mean, I didn't know if you were really coming. I hadn't heard from you…" Her voice trailed off then her stance changed as she pushed her shoulders back and the set of her mouth tightened. Her gaze shifted to the dress he was holding up, and her eyes narrowed. "Nice dress. Does it belong to your date?"

"My *date*?" His glance flicked to the dress then back to Lorna as he shook his head at the absurdity of the idea that he would bring a date to this event when she was the only woman he couldn't seem to get out of his mind. It also seemed crazy, judging by the style of the dress, that she thought he would be dating a woman old enough to be his grandmother. "No, this was in the garment bag labeled with my name. There must have been a mix-up." He dropped the dress and grabbed the new white T-shirt that had also been on the bed. "What do you need help with?"

"What?" she asked, her gaze locked on his chest as he pulled the shirt on. She shook her head, as if to clear it, then waved away his question. "Oh, it's nothing. Never mind." Her expression hardened again as she turned to go. "I'll find Ford."

"You've already found me," he said, taking a step towards her. "And you know I care about Chevy and Leni. You said there was a problem. I'd like to help, if I can."

She turned back to him. He wasn't sure what was causing all the animosity, but there were definitely waves of iciness in the glare she directed at him. The temperature outside was already warm for late spring, but it was downright chilly in this room.

She held his gaze, and he could practically see her mind weighing the options of accepting his offer to help versus continuing to search for Ford.

Her shoulders fell, then once it seemed her mind

was made up, her words came out in a panicky rush. "The guy who was bringing the convertible that was supposed to drive Leni out to the meadow where the wedding is set up just called, and he can't come. He said either his kid or his cow was sick. Not that it matters. I mean, of course, I don't want his kid to be sick. *Or* his cow. But, once he said he wasn't coming, I couldn't really hear anything over the blood rushing in my ears."

Okay. This didn't seem like a total emergency and definitely didn't warrant the frantic tone of Lorna's voice. "Can't she just walk out to the meadow?"

Lorna raised an eyebrow in an expression that smacked of pure *'you're an idiot'* vibes. "Not in the heels she's wearing *or* dragging that gorgeous dress."

"Got it," he said, thoroughly chastised. "So, we need a new way to get her from the house to the meadow?"

Lorna nodded. "Correct."

"Well, I can drive her," he offered, although his truck was covered in highway dust and bug guts from the drive from Texas.

Lorna shook her head. "She wouldn't fit. Well, *she* would fit, but the dress wouldn't. It's got a long train and needs lots of open space around it. The convertible was perfect."

Open space around it? How long was this train? Like the Trans-Siberian Railway?

"What about one of the tractors?" he offered.

Her brow arched even higher, apparently either confirming or amplifying his earlier 'idiot' status. "My sister is *not* arriving to her fairy tale wedding on a tractor."

He tried to think of how a woman *would* want to arrive to a fairy tale wedding.

"This is the first wedding I've ever been to, so I'm not sure what the hell a fairy tale wedding even means," he told her. "Like a princess marrying a prince?" He tried to imagine his all-cowboy brother, who primarily wore jeans, boots, and T-shirts, in royal carb riding a gallant steed.

"You've never attended a wedding?" Lorna asked. "I've been to a million. And yes, every bride imagines herself as a princess."

An idea suddenly came to him. "I know," he said, reaching for a fresh pair of socks and his good cowboy boots and yanking them both on. "Follow me," he told her, leading the way down the hall and out the front door.

The farmhouse was a large rambling two-story that sat nestled against a backdrop of tall mountains. The stone and wood exterior with huge windows looking out over the ranch gave it a cabin-type feel, and the long wrap around porch had been the location of many sunrise cups of coffee and sunset glasses of iced tea or cold beer.

The huge white barn with the Lassiter brand painted on the front sat across from the house. Corrals extended off either side, and two of his brother's horses stood calmly munching hay as they watched Mack and Lorna race across the yard. White fences ran along both sides of the driveway, enclosing green pastures, and several hundred head of cattle could be seen dotting the grassland leading up into the mountainside beyond the house.

A chicken coop and vegetable garden sat off to the

right of the house, neat rows of spring plants already showing tiny bits of growth. The ranch was well-taken care of, all the Lassiter men took pride in it and worked hard to maintain its upkeep.

This place had taken in three boys whom no one had wanted, and Mack wished he would have had a chance to meet the grandmother who had raised his brothers.

He was the only one who had been raised by their mother, but there were lots of ways to abandon a child, and Mack had come searching for the family he'd never known the summer before, not knowing if they would accept or reject him. His brothers, and their grandfather, Duke, had taken him into the fold as one of their own, and he'd fallen in love with the Lassiter ranch and the mountains of Colorado.

He just wished he wouldn't have had to leave it, and the woman hurrying to keep up with him, so soon and for so long. But he was back for good now, and that was all that mattered.

He led Lorna down the alley of the barn then stopped in front of a stall holding a large white horse. "Would Leni arriving on a white horse count for like something from a fairy tale wedding?"

Lorna's eyes widened, and her voice came out as a hushed whisper. "Wow. He's beautiful. And perfect." She turned her gaze back to Mack. "Where did he come from? Who does he belong to?"

"He's mine." He reached his hand over the stall door and the horse nuzzled his palm. "Lorna, I'd like you to meet Zeus. The best friend any guy could ask for."

"Hi Zeus," she said, giving the horse's neck a pat.

"You are beautiful." She arched an eyebrow at Mack. "I never pictured you as a white horse kind-of-guy."

He'd never considered himself one either. "I am most definitely *not* a white horse kind-of-guy, and I've never been accused of being one. And technically, Zeus is gray. He's just such a light gray that he looks white. If that helps erase that image from your mind."

She narrowed her eyes, as if trying to figure out something about him, then turned back to the horse. "He's perfect. Leni will love riding up to the wedding on his back. Are you sure it's okay for her to use him?"

He nodded. "Heck yeah. He—*and I*—would be honored." He nodded toward the tack room just inside the barn door. "I can have him saddled and ready to go in about ten minutes."

"Great. I'll go find something to fancy him up a bit," she said over her shoulder as she turned and hurried from the barn. "Be back in five."

Mack had the horse saddled and ready by the time Lorna came rushing back into the barn carrying a tote bag overflowing with blue and silver décor.

"I don't know how you're planning to *fancy* him up," he said. "But I gave him a quick brush and hooked a saddle bag around the saddle horn in case Leni needs a place to hold her bouquet while she gets on and off the horse."

"That's genius. Do you think Zeus would mind terribly if I braided a few of these into his mane?" she asked, holding up a handful of silver and blue ribbons.

Mack laughed. "Nah. He's pretty secure in his manhood. I think he can handle it." He brushed out the horse's tail as Lorna twisted ribbons and silk flowers into his mane, the silver and blue decorations blending perfectly with his light gray coat.

He tried to keep his focus on the horse, he knew they were under a time crunch, but he kept getting distracted by the scent of Lorna's hair and the softness of her skin every time she brushed past him.

They'd spent quite a bit of time together when he'd first come to town, but they'd usually been in a group setting with the whole Lassiter clan. This might be the first time he'd been alone with her, and he was suddenly nervous.

He'd thought she was pretty from the first day he'd met her, but this afternoon, with her hair swept up and in the silky silver-blue dress that was the same color as her eyes, she was staggering.

And he couldn't seem to think of a single intelligent thing to say.

They'd had a comfortable flirty rapport from the start, but it had seemed easier to tease and joke around with her when she was barefoot or wearing jean shorts and one of her funny T-shirts that usually read something about how much she loved reading and coffee.

Now, she just seemed way out of his league.

Not that it mattered. She'd specifically told him she only wanted to be friends before he'd left, so there was no reason to be nervous. But his palms were still sweating, and his brain was still refusing to give him any clever conversational crumbs.

"I'll text Leni and tell her we'll meet her by the front porch," Lorna said, breaking into his thoughts. "I already told her the convertible was a no-show, but I promised she'd love this idea more."

"I hope you're right," he said, picking up the reins and leading the horse out of the barn.

"My sister may be a rocket scientist and a total brainiac nerd. But she's still a sucker for romance. And she's going to love riding up to the ceremony on a white horse."

Lorna was right.

The front door opened as they walked up to the porch, and Eleanor (Leni) Gibbs, the bride-to-be, stepped out in a beautiful flowing white dress. A huge smile broke across her face, and she opened her arms as she walked down the steps toward them.

"Mack, I'm so glad you made it." She pulled him into a tight hug. "It's so good to see you."

"It's good to see you, too," Mack said, still not quite used to the easy affection shared among the Lassiter's and their partners. All his brother's girlfriends had accepted him, and the whole bunch of them had drawn him right into the family. "Congratulations."

"Thank you. I couldn't be happier to be marrying your brother." She beamed a broad smile at him then turned her attention to Zeus. "Wow. He's gorgeous. Where'd he come from?"

"He's mine," Mack told her. "I brought him back from Texas with me. You sure you're okay riding him? He's not quite as impressive as a convertible."

"He's perfect. Lorna was worried about the car not being here, but this is a thousand times better." She leaned into him and lowered her voice. "And to be honest, I don't care all that much about *how* I get to the meadow—as long as I get there. If you all wouldn't have found a solution, I would have just taken these fancy shoes off and raced barefoot to the altar."

"You'll do no such thing," Lorna told her as she spread a large blue tablecloth across the saddle. "I thought you could sit on this. I found it in Duke's kitchen, so it's something borrowed *and* something blue."

Mack pulled the horse up to the steps and helped Leni into the saddle.

She hooked one knee over the pommel to affect a side-saddle position. "This is great," she told him as he tucked her bouquet into the saddle bag hanging next to her. "I love it."

Lorna pulled a blue button-down shirt and a navy tie from the depths of the tote bag and passed them to Mack. "I didn't have time to track down your wedding clothes, so this was the best I could do. I found this stuff in Chevy's closet."

"It's great. Thanks." He pulled the shirt on and quickly buttoned it as Lorna fussed with Leni's dress, spreading it out to lay perfectly around her legs and the saddle.

He ran into the house and grabbed the gray cowboy hat that had been left for him on the kitchen table then looked up at Leni as he finished knotting the tie he'd slipped around his neck. "Is this okay? I don't want to mess up the look of the wedding. I can stay in the back if you want."

"Don't you dare," Leni told him. "Chevy wants all *three* of his brothers standing up there with him. Lorna told me your outfit got mixed up with someone else, but this is close enough, and really, no one will care or probably even notice."

"They won't notice me because no one will be able to take their eyes off the gorgeous bride," he told her, appreciating the comment about Chevy wanting *all* his brothers with him enough to ignore the fact she'd just called his clothes an *outfit*.

In his world, an outfit was his pickup and trailer, *not* his clothing choice.

"Thank you. You're sweet," Leni said. "Now, if you two are done fussing around, let's go get me married. The ceremony is starting any minute, and you're supposed to be walking up the aisle first," she told Lorna.

"All right, I'll go, if you're sure you're okay," Lorna said, still holding on to Leni's leg.

"I'm fine. I trust Mack." Leni smiled down at him. "He'll take good care of me."

Mack nodded, a rush of pride at her comment warming his chest. "Absolutely."

"Okay, I'll see you at the altar. I love you, Sister," Lorna called over her shoulder as she hiked up her dress and hurried toward the meadow where the ceremony was set up.

Mack smoothed the front of his shirt. Of the four half-brothers, he and Chevy looked the most like each other and had the same build, so the shirt fit as if he'd bought it for himself. Ford and Dodge both had blondish hair, but Chevy and Mack must have gotten their dark hair from their mother's side of the family.

Their mother had a lot of problems, like being a drunk and making the poor decision to name her four sons after the types of trucks that each of their dead-beat dads had driven away from them in—oh, and then abandoning three of them—but she was a gorgeous woman and had passed the Lassiter good looks to all four of her sons.

The ceremony was set up in the meadow with the best view of the mountains behind it, which put it on the other side of the barn and made it so the guests couldn't see the house from where they sat. So, he and Leni had to walk around the far edge of the barn to get to it.

The light strains of piano music filled the air as they saw Lorna disappear around the side of the barn. Mack recognized the song as "It's Your Love" by Faith Hill and Tim McGraw.

He took hold of Zeus's reins and smiled up at Leni. "You ready?"

Chapter Two

MACK COULDN'T IMAGINE a more radiant smile than the one Leni flashed down at him.

"If you don't start walking, I might grab the reins and gallop this horse to the altar," she teased.

"Let's go then," Mack said, laughing as he imagined Leni charging down the aisle on the huge white horse.

He led the horse across the driveway then paused at the corner of the barn, not sure how to proceed.

"We won't go until the song ends and they start playing the traditional "Wedding March"," Leni told him. "But you can peek around the corner to see if it looks like they're ready."

Mack stuck his head around the side of the barn and caught his breath at the sight of the meadow in the faded light of dusk, the mountains rising behind it. Every evergreen tree twinkled with tiny white fairy lights, and bouquets of purple lupine stalks were tied to the sides of the chairs lining the center walkway.

Hundreds of chairs were set up in the freshly mown grass making a vast emerald-green carpet beneath them. A simple arch constructed of cedar planks stood at the front, adorned with more twinkling evergreen boughs, white roses, and a wooden sign that read, "Love Abides Here".

Under the arch stood his brother, Chevy, looking excited and happy and not one bit nervous. Next to him were Ford and Dodge. They all wore jeans, square-toed brown leather cowboy boots, blue button-downs with silver vests, navy ties, and gray felt cowboy hats. At least Mack had the same hat, jeans, and boots. His shirt was a little lighter shade of blue and he didn't have a matching vest, but he didn't think he'd mess up the aesthetic too much.

And between how gorgeous Leni looked and the array of beautiful women in silvery blue dresses on the bride's side, no one would even notice him. Ford's girlfriend, Elizabeth Cole, and Dodge's girlfriend, Maisie Graham, were already standing at the front, facing the audience, and Lorna had just taken her place next to them and turned around.

"How does it look?" Leni whispered from her perch on the tall horse. "Did my groom show up?"

"You mean the guy standing at the altar with the goofy grin on his face?"

"Yeah, that's him," she said, her own grin bursting across her face. Then her brow furrowed. "Are any of the chairs filled? I think we put almost everyone we know in the wedding party."

Mack laughed. "It looks like most of the town of Woodland Hills is here. I'm not sure if there's even one empty chair."

"You're kidding?" She twisted her hands together. "Shoot, now I'm suddenly nervous. Mack, do *not* let me fall off this horse."

"I won't. I promise," he told her as the last chorus of the song started, which Lorna had told him was their cue to walk in. "You ready to marry my brother?" It had been nine months since he'd found his family, but it still sometimes felt weird to use the term 'brother'.

Leni didn't notice as she pushed her shoulders back and sat up straighter in the saddle. "I've been ready to marry Chevy Lassiter for most of my life. Wild horses couldn't keep me away."

He clucked his tongue, and Zeus fell into step next to him as he kept one hand securely on Leni's leg, keeping his promise to not let her fall, and led them around the corner of the barn.

A collective gasp went up from the wedding guests at the vision of the gorgeous bride astride the huge white horse. Chevy's face lit with wonder and delight, but Mack wasn't sure if he even noticed the horse.

He only had eyes for Leni.

And the sight of the love shining there had emotion suddenly burning Mack's throat.

He smoothed down the front of his shirt and led the horse toward the silver runner where Duke was waiting, his eyes also shining with love for his new granddaughter-in-law. He tried not to think about the several hundred people from Woodland Hills who were watching them approach and either wondering who he was or judging his mother for abandoning another son, born out of wedlock and given a ridiculous name.

Stop. He tried to convince himself they were all looking at the bride and that no one was paying him any attention, but he spotted a few wayward glances directed his way.

He caught the eye of Dodge, who smiled like he was happy to see him, and Duke gave him a giant bear hug as he made it to the end of the runner. That was all Mack needed.

He didn't give a crap what this town, or anyone else thought of him, as long as these men accepted him. It had been so long since he'd felt wanted or cared about by anyone resembling family.

"Good to see you, Son," Duke said, beaming at him as he released him with a clap on the back. Matt couldn't help but grin back. He'd only discovered the existence of his half-brothers and his grandparents the year before, but Mack had loved Duke from the moment he'd met him.

Everyone loved Duke. He was an old cowboy with a hearty laugh, a warm personality, and a penchant for baking cookies and the perfect pie crust. In his mid-seventies, and thanks to all those pies and cookies, he had a bit more of a belly than he used to, but he was still tall and strong as an ox. With his pure white hair, full beard, and a wide mustache, he looked like a cross between Sam Elliott and Santa Claus.

Duke was dressed in the same fashion as his grandsons, but the white rose boutonniere tucked in his lapel designated his role as Chevy's best man, and Mack couldn't have chosen a better guy for the job. Duke Lassiter was the best man he knew.

Mack reached up to help Leni down from the horse then passed her hand to his grandfather, who would walk her down the aisle. He gave her the bouquet then stepped away to wrap the ends of the reins around the corral post next to the meadow and pat Zeus's neck as he quietly told him to 'stay'. The ceremony wouldn't be long, and the horse was used to waiting.

He turned to head down the aisle. He was out of order, but glancing at the bridal party, he realized he would've been the odd man out, walking down the aisle by himself, anyway. Maybe he should have had Zeus accompany him instead of tying him to a post.

Yeah, that would be way less conspicuous than just walking by himself.

A tiny, adorable flower girl, with bouncy blond curls and a frilly dress, had just made her way down the aisle, dropping pink and white rose petals in clumps as she went. Murphy, Chevy's English Cream golden retriever trotted protectively by her side, a silver vest on his back, claiming the title, "Best Dog".

Lorna's son, Max, was making his way down the aisle behind her, but must have realized he had a captive audience, because he stopped in the middle and took advantage of the spotlight as he proceeded to do several dance moves, including the running man and the floss. Two gold rings, hopefully not the real wedding ones, were attached by ribbons to a satin pillow, which Max was now swinging around his head like a helicopter blade.

Mack wasn't sure if the five-year-old—no, now six—he'd had a birthday last month and Mack had bought him a Lego set for it that was still tucked into the back of his truck, would even recognize him.

Lorna had just taken a step towards her son, a tight smile of embarrassment on her face, when Max turned and saw Mack. The boy's small face lit with recognition as he dropped the pillow—yeah, Mack *really* hoped those weren't the real rings—and ran full out toward him, his arms outstretched. "Mack! You're back!" he shouted as Mack bent to scoop him up into a hug.

Those dang emotions were burning his throat again as Max's small arms wrapped around his neck.

Chapter Three

LORNA GIBBS—SHE *HAD* taken her maiden name, and hopefully some of her dignity, back after the divorce—stared open-mouthed at her son.

Leni and Lorna's family had been absorbed into the Lassiter clan around the same time Mack had first shown up in town, searching for the half-brothers he'd just found out about. They'd all spent a lot of time together, for family dinners and football games, and she and Mack had shared some flirty moments.

She liked the handsome cowboy. He was kind and thoughtful, and respectful to his grandfather, and to her. She relished his attention and his sweet compliments, but she'd been smack-dab in the middle of a divorce and had a brand-new baby to boot when they'd first met. She'd just broken her ankle and was so tired, she felt like she could barely form a coherent sentence, let alone start up some kind of romance with a hot cowboy, no matter how tall and muscly his broad chest was.

She'd known that her sweet son, Max, had liked the cowboy, too. He liked all the Lassiter men. They treated him so differently than his own father had.

Lyle either ignored the boy or chastised him for being too loud or too talkative or for not picking up his toys.

But Duke and Chevy and his brothers all loved Max, taking him along to do chores or for rides on the tractor. And Mack was the first to agree to play a game or build Lego stuff with him, getting down on the floor with the boy, and having real conversations where he actually listened to the stories Max loved to tell. Mack had bought him his first pair of cowboy boots, and Max had practically slept in them.

They had all missed Mack when he'd gotten called back to help at the ranch in Texas where he'd worked before, but he'd said he would only be gone for a few weeks. Then the foreman of the ranch had broken his leg, and then they'd needed him for winter calving, and then something else had happened, and then something else, and suddenly he'd been gone months instead of weeks.

They hadn't gotten to the point of talking to each other on the phone, but they had been texting and sending each other funny reels. Then once he left, his texts had dwindled from frequent to sporadic to non-existent. Which, she tried to convince herself, was fine with her. She had enough on her plate trying to pay her bills and keep up with the laundry and dishes while running her coffee shop, Mountain Brew, and raising a rambunctious kindergartener and a nine-month-old baby girl who was getting ready to walk.

When Mack had first left, he was all Max talked about, but after several months, the boy had stopped mentioning his name. Lorna wasn't sure if he'd just forgotten about the cowboy or if he'd assumed Mack had simply left him behind, just like his father had done.

But the way Max had just called his name and gone racing into Mack's arms told her the boy hadn't forgotten him. She swallowed, hard, at the burn of emotion clogging her throat from seeing the tall cowboy hug her boy to his chest and laugh as he ruffled his hair.

Mack kept the boy in his arms as he continued down the aisle, stopping to scoop up the dropped ring pillow, then greeting his brothers with hugs and handshakes before taking his place at the end of the line.

He caught her eye and grinned as he nodded to the front row of guests where Mabel Turner, a petite elderly lady who had been one of Duke's wife's best friends, was wearing black slacks and a much-too-big-for-her blue shirt, belted with a navy necktie and covered by a large silver vest.

She stifled a giggle. Apparently, they'd just solved the mystery of the culprit whose garment bag had been mixed up with Mack's.

So, the dress really *hadn't* belonged to his date.

And she felt surprisingly happy about that fact.

Then the "Wedding March" began to play, and she let go of her thoughts about the hot cowboy as she turned to watch her beautiful sister, a broad smile on her face and her arm threaded through the elbow of Duke, as Leni walked down the aisle and toward the love of her life.

She'd never seen her older sister so happy.

Leni was getting married, and to the man of her dreams. Tears filled Lorna's eyes as she listened to them recite their heartfelt vows, and she fulfilled her maid of honor duties, holding the bouquet while they exchanged rings—thankfully the real ones had been in Duke's pocket instead of being flung along the aisle in her son's impromptu dance party—but her gaze kept straying to the man on the other side of the aisle who her son was standing next to and staring up at with the rapt devotion of a golden retriever puppy.

She'd spent the last seven months trying to convince herself he wasn't *that* good-looking, or that tall, or that kind. She'd been wrong.

He was even hotter than she'd remembered.

His muscled chest and jet-black hair had her heart pounding against her chest and her insides tumbling around like towels in a dryer.

When she'd stormed into Ford's room earlier, her heart had nearly stopped at the sight of Mack, barefoot, in jeans and a white T-shirt clinging to his broad chest, his tousled hair, still wet from the shower and curling at his neck.

She'd set up a million scenarios in her head of when she would see him again, and was beyond thrilled that she'd had makeup on, her hair done and was dressed to the nines versus wearing day old mascara and her usual outfit of yoga pants and a questionably clean shirt that was likely stained with either coffee or some flavor of baby food.

He'd looked at her in a way she hadn't been looked at in a long time. And he'd said she looked '*stunning*'. That one word—a description her ex had *never* uttered—went straight into her heart and buried itself there like a treasure inside a chest she could pull out later to hold and cherish.

Her attention sprang back to her sister as the minister proclaimed, "By the power vested in me by the state of Colorado, I now pronounce you husband and wife. You may kiss the bride."

She laughed and held back a sob of happiness—and a little grief over remembering her own failed marriage vows—as Chevy grabbed Leni and bent her back in an exaggerated dip before pressing his lips to hers in a passionate kiss.

He pulled her back to standing as he let out a whoop then kissed her again. Joy radiated off both him and Leni, like a campfire giving off warmth and light, and making everyone around them lean in, as if wanting to capture some of that happiness for themselves.

Lorna couldn't have been happier for her older sister. Leni had stepped in and taken care of her when their father had left and their mother had fallen apart, and Lorna knew that her sister had fallen in love with Chevy Lassiter the moment she'd laid eyes on him.

But there was a tiny feeling, like a small worm in an otherwise delicious apple, that had her glancing over at Mack and wondering if she'd ever get to feel that kind of love. If she'd ever be brave enough to risk getting her heart shattered and stomped on and tossed away like a fast-food wrapper again.

She felt a nudge in her back from Elizabeth, the bridesmaid behind her, and realized Duke was waiting to walk back down the aisle with her. Lunging forward, she smiled at her sister's new grandfather-in-law and tried to put thoughts of handsome cowboys and shattered hearts behind her.

It was Leni's day, *and* the first night she'd been out

without Isabel, in months, and she was determined to enjoy it.

Maisie's neighbor, Gertie Henderson, who was a mother of five, a grandmother to eight, and a great-grandmother to two, had offered to stay overnight at Lorna's house to watch Izzy, so Lorna could participate in all the wedding festivities.

Gertie had been watching Izzy a few days a week while Lorna worked at the coffee shop. The little girl loved her bonus grandma, and it meant everything to Lorna to know her baby was with someone she could trust.

"Mom," Max called as he and Mack made it to the end of the aisle runner. He ran to her and threw his arms around her legs as he flashed a huge grin up at her. "Did you see that Mack is back? And he brought me a birthday present. Even though he missed my birthday. But he said he was real sorry he wasn't back in time to see me and have some of my birthday cake, which I told him had the Teenage Mutant Ninja Turtles on it so the frosting turned your tongue green and black. And he said that sounded really cool."

"Okay, slow down, take a breath, buddy," she told him, used to her son's mile-a-minute conversation style, and wondering when he and Mack had time to discuss Max's birthday party and the black and green frosting—which had been more disgusting than cool, in her opinion, but it had made Max happy, and so it had been worth it.

And had Mack really bought Max a birthday gift?

If he had, it would have been more than her ex had done. Lyle had called her a few days after, full of excuses and justifications of why he'd missed his own son's birthday and asked her to stick a twenty in a card and sign his name to it. Which she'd already done the night of his birthday, not for Lyle, but so Max didn't have to know what a shit-heel his father was.

Not that Max was short on gifts. The Lassiter clan had held his birthday party at the ranch, offering pony rides and ice cream to the few friends he'd invited, and had showered him with presents and hugs. But still, it sucked that his own father had forgotten.

And it meant something that Mack hadn't. He had texted that day and sent Max a funny GIF of a tiny dog scarfing down a huge birthday cake. Her son had loved it.

"Hey," Mack said, catching up to Max and obviously hearing the tail end of their conversation. "I hope it's okay that I got him a gift. I probably should have checked with you first, but he was telling me about his birthday, and it slipped out that I had brought him something back from Texas."

"It's fine," she told him, surprised, and a little curious, about what he'd had the foresight to purchase and bring with him from the Lone Star state. "As long as it isn't one of those cows you've been taking care of."

Mack's face fell. "Oh dang. They told me I couldn't return it." Then he smiled as he teased her.

She lifted one shoulder in a good-natured shrug. "Well, I guess I *will* have a spare bedroom now that Leni's moving out and into the cabin at the lake with Chevy."

Max jumped up and down, pure glee evident in his grin. "Am I really getting a cow? And I can keep it in Aunt Leni's room? I promise I'll feed it every day.

And take it for walks. And it can even sleep in my bed, if it wants."

Oops.

"No, I'm sorry, honey. Mack and I were just teasing each other. He didn't really bring you a cow back from Texas." She glanced up at him, a question in her eyes, and dropped her shoulders in relief when he grinned then shook his head.

Max's body sagged against her as if his bones had all turned to spaghetti. "Aww dang. I would have really liked having my own cow. Can you think about it for when I turn seven?"

"Sure, buddy," she said, giving his limp body a hug.

"I need to get Zeus back to the barn and take his saddle off. How about you come help me, then we'll visit some of the cows on our way to my truck to get your gift?" Mack asked, then glanced back at Lorna. "I mean, if that's okay with your mom."

Lorna nodded. "Sure. Just don't take too long. And *don't get dirty*. Aunt Leni wants us *all* for pictures in fifteen minutes. Including you," she told Mack. "Why don't I try to track down Mabel Turner and see if I trade her dress for your wedding clothes, so you'll at least have the right ones for the pictures."

Ten minutes later, she met Mack and her son in the kitchen of the ranch house, his shirt, tie, and vest hanging over her arm.

"Mom, look at this huge present Mack got for me," Max told her, gesturing to the rather large box sitting on the kitchen table. "Can I open it now?" he asked, already ripping into the paper almost before she told him he could.

He tore the wrapping paper away—another

impressive thing that Mack had the foresight to not only bring a gift, but to wrap it in blue and white paper covered in the Paw Patrol puppies—to reveal a Lego set for a huge pirate ship. "This is sooo cool. I love it just as much as a cow," Max said, jumping down from the chair and throwing himself into Mack's arms. "Thank you, Mack. Will you help me build it? Can we do it now?"

"I'm glad you like it," Mack said. "I always wanted one of these when I was a kid." Lorna noticed a shadow of sadness darken Mack's eyes, then it disappeared so quickly, she wondered if she'd seen it at all. "And I'd be happy to help you build it, but tonight is all about your Aunt Leni and your new Uncle Chevy and celebrating their wedding, so we'll have to make a plan for another day."

Max's mouth turned down in a frown then he lifted his eyebrows. "How about tomorrow?"

Mack laughed and the sound of it did something funny to Lorna's insides. Not just the rich sound of his laughter, but the fact that it was her son who was bringing him genuine joy. She couldn't remember ever hearing Lyle laugh like that with him.

"We'll have to check with your mom on that one," Mack said.

Max's head whipped toward her, but before she could answer, Mabel Turner came down the hallway wearing the silver dress that had been left on Ford's bed.

"Well, I must admit," she said. "This does seem like a more reasonable choice for wedding attire. I wasn't sure what to do when I opened my garment bag earlier and found those other clothes, but I was already at the ranch and didn't have anything else to wear, so as they say in my Zumba class, I just went with it and made the best of a bad dance move."

Chapter Four

Mack had to admit that he felt more like part of the family once he'd changed into the same wedding shirt and vest that his brothers and grandfather were wearing. He was thankful Lorna had gotten his things back from Miss Mabel, and the older woman seemed glad too.

The pictures took close to an hour, so the reception was well underway by the time they made it to the giant white tent set up in the pasture on the other side of the barn.

The white chairs had been moved from the ceremony to circle round tables covered in silver tablecloths, and the lupine stalks had been transformed into centerpieces. Chandeliers of fairy lights hung from the tent's crossbeams, and a head table had been set up for the bridal party with a banner reading 'Mr. and Mrs. Lassiter' strung behind it.

Animated conversation, laughter, and the scent of pulled pork and barbequed brisket filled the air, and long tables held massive bowls of potato salad, cole slaw, baked beans, macaroni and cheese, salad, grilled corn on the cob, and freshly made rolls. Huge coolers had been filled with ice and stuffed with beer, ciders, hard seltzers, soda, and water.

The wedding party got in line and filled their plates then took their places at the head table. Mack had been hoping to sit with Lorna, but her place as the maid of honor was already set next to Leni, and he had been assigned a seat at the end of the table next to Dodge. He was glad to get to catch up a little with his brother, but it seemed like half the town came up to the table to talk to the bride and groom and the rest of the family.

Mack lost track of how many people he'd been introduced to. Some of the neighbors, and the friends of his grandparents, he'd met when he'd been there the summer before, but a lot of folks were new. And many seemed curious about him, his mom, and how he'd come to recently join the Lassiter family.

He appreciated Dodge's skills at evading the questions that got too personal and his knack for changing the subject and putting the focus back on the other person. Especially since Mack didn't have good answers to some of their questions. Like why his mom had chosen to keep him with her when she'd abandoned the other boys with their grandparents and why she'd never told him about his half-brothers.

After the meal, he was happy to find an out-of-the-way spot to hold up the wall as he watched Chevy and Leni cut the cake and do the garter and bouquet tosses.

Duke had told him most of the crowd was either from Woodland Hills or the neighboring town of Creedence, and even though he'd heard he was from the area, Mack was still surprised to see NHL hockey legend, Rockford James and his brothers in attendance and tipping beers with *his* new brothers. He loved watching the guy play and was a fan of his team, the Colorado Summit, so he hoped to get a chance to get to know Rock and the James brothers better this summer since Duke said they occasionally helped each other out on their respective ranches.

Mack didn't participate in the garter toss, and he was amused at the way Lorna didn't even *try* to catch the bouquet, side-stepping the direction of Leni's throw instead then laughing with a surprised Miss Mabel as the flowers landed in her arms.

He'd always been okay circling the periphery, watching others, and never needing to join in to whatever activity was going on. Especially since he hadn't been invited to join much. And making friends and getting too close to people invited questions he didn't want to answer, like about where his mom was and why they hadn't seen her around.

He'd learned early on that answering those questions truthfully only brought trouble, so he'd become good at doing his own laundry to ensure he had clean clothes, learning to use coupons and make himself inexpensive meals, and forging his mother's signatures on notes for school, so that no one suspected Brandy had taken off again, leaving her young son alone for weeks, and sometimes months at a time.

The band played a song for the couple's first dance but skipped the father/daughter and mother and son ones, since neither the bride nor groom had either parent in attendance. Leni and Lorna's father had taken off on them when they were young, and their mother had remarried and moved away the summer before and apparently hadn't made it back for the wedding.

Mack didn't think Brandi would have been invited, even if any of them knew where she was, and he was the only Lassiter son who'd even known his dad, although he sure didn't consider himself luckier in that respect.

He still couldn't believe this was all part of his life now. He'd spent his entire life wishing for siblings and grandparents, heck, he would have taken a distant cousin, just to know he had some other family out there. But he'd never imagined that he had three brothers and a grandfather on a ranch in Colorado.

Or that they would so easily accept him as one of their own.

They *had* accepted him, but standing there, on the perimeter of the party, he couldn't help but still feel alone.

This ranch was his home now. He'd told the ranch foreman in Texas he wasn't coming back again. But it was still going to take him some time to really adjust to this ranch being part of his legacy and to these people being his family.

He watched for a few songs then couldn't turn down Elizabeth or Maisie's requests to dance, even though he knew they were just asking him to be nice to their boyfriend's little brother.

Lorna had been having a great night, enjoying the freedom of being able to eat a warm meal with other adults and knowing Izzy was home with a babysitter she could trust. She'd danced a few times with Max, then with Duke, then been hustled onto the floor by her sister for the group line dances. She was surprised she remembered the steps, but after a few mistakes, seemed to easily pick them back up again.

She'd been hoping to have a dance with Mack, feeling like this was her one Cinderella night out and at midnight she'd turn back into a single-working-mom pumpkin, leaving the memories of a pretty dress and a gorgeous updo behind like the lost glass slipper.

It was close to nine when Mack finally asked her to dance, but her pulse quickened when the music changed to a slower number as he led her out onto the floor and pulled her into his arms.

His hand rested gently against her shoulder blade as he guided her around the floor, but all she could think about was the feel of his fingers brushing over the bare skin next to the thin straps of her dress and how well she fit against his broad chest.

His breath tickled her ear as he leaned down to talk to her, making her laugh as he told her how Miss Bernie, an elderly local woman who Leni and Chevy had befriended the year before when they'd returned her lost cow, Babydoll, had walked over to the wedding so she could bring that same cow with her to attend the nuptials and then asked for a stall to keep her in, as if the wedding provided a bovine valet service.

She knew that the night wasn't real, that in the morning she'd go back to her yoga pants, and never-ending piles of laundry, and dirty diapers, and pans of dried macaroni and cheese, but tonight was for pretending she was still beautiful and desirable to a hot cowboy with hard abs and a rakish grin.

Not that her life was all bad.

She loved being a mom and found joy in playing games with and reading stories to Max and singing endless rounds of silly songs to make Izzy giggle, but sometimes she got so tired and missed the feeling of simply being a woman.

And spinning around the dance floor in Mack Lassiter's arms had her feeling not only *like* a woman but had her woman parts tingling and feeling sensations she hadn't experienced in a long time. Since about nine months ago, around the same time she'd first met him.

They'd really had fun together then, and at times, had flirted shamelessly with each other. Then he left and essentially ghosted her. Although tonight she had felt like he was flirting again and there was no way she was imagining those looks he kept casting her way.

He must have caught her frown, because he pulled her closer and spoke into the ear. "What's up? Your face just flipped through fifteen expressions in five seconds, like it was a Viewmaster on crack."

A grin tugged at the corners of her lips. "Leni has always accused me of wearing my heart on my sleeves. She says she can always tell what I'm thinking."

"Well, I don't have that benefit, so you're gonna have to tell me. What's going on? You looked happy then sad then kind of mad."

She peered up at him, loving that she could wear heels and still have him taller than her, and studied his face.

Did he really want her to answer honestly? Most men preferred to hear what they wanted to hear. But, even in the short time she'd known him, Mack had proved to be different than most men.

"I was just thinking about why you stopped texting me while you were gone. It felt like you were ghosting me."

His brow furrowed. "I'm sorry for that. Life on a ranch is tough. Especially when you're short-handed. I was working long, hard hours from sun-up to sun-down and most nights, I barely got my boots off before falling into bed. That's if I had a bed to fall into. We spent plenty of nights in the pasture sleeping with the herd. I'm not making excuses, just offering an explanation. And honestly, I wasn't sure you wanted me to keep texting you."

"Why would you think that?"

"Because when I was here before, it seemed like you were into me, then a few nights before I left, the night we had that big barbeque at the ranch, you told me you just wanted to be friends."

Lorna tried to think back to that night. "I remember that barbeque and sitting out on the deck feeling utterly exhausted by the end of the meal. Izzy had been fussy and wouldn't let anyone else hold her, and Max had missed his nap that day and dumped an entire bowl of barbeque sauce into his lap. And I'd been trying to get inventory done for the coffee shop that week, so I was feeling mad and sad and cranky that I had to do everything by myself."

"I didn't know any of that. So, did I make things worse by coming over to sit with you?"

She shook her head. "No, not at all. I actually remember you sitting down next to me and offering to take Izzy." She pressed a hand to her chest. "I can almost feel that sweaty warm spot on my chest where she'd been laying most of the night and the relief I'd felt as you took her, and she let you cuddle her on your shoulder. I don't recall exactly what you said, but it was something flirty, and all I could think about was what a hot mess I was, going through a divorce, near tears, barely holding it together, and I think I responded with something like what I really needed was a friend."

It was his turn to study her. "So, maybe I took your comment out of context?"

She shrugged. "I don't know. Maybe. Or maybe it was exactly what you were thinking. I know that I *did* need a friend then. And I still do."

"I didn't realize you were going through all that. But it sounds like I wasn't a very good friend when you needed it." He raised a questioning eyebrow. "Would you give me another chance to be a better one?"

She smiled, liking and respecting that he wasn't making excuses or gaslighting her into thinking his ghosting her was all her fault.

"I'm still a hot mess," she told him. "I get cranky and still cry for what feels like no reason but is usually triggered by someone vomiting or a poop blowout or too many freaking piles of laundry and never enough time to vacuum. But if you're up for all that, I can always use another friend."

He offered her one of those rakish grins she'd remembered so well. "Count me in. Hot messes are my favorite kind."

He was smiling when he said it, but the look he was giving her was a panty-melting smolder. And she couldn't tear her gaze from his.

Leaning closer, he lowered his voice as he spoke next to her ear. "Although I don't know if I agree so much with the mess, but I'll definitely go along with the *hot* part."

She let out a laugh—she had to. It was either that or rip her dress off and yell *'take me now'*. His voice was like how she imagined warm whiskey mixed with honey would feel sliding down her throat—something sweet and sexy that she could get drunk on.

She let him pull her closer.

Words failed her, but she felt like she had to say something.

"I like that you make me laugh," she told him.

There. That was sort of flirty but could also fit in the realm of friends, which is where she'd essentially just told him she wanted to stay.

But she also liked being in the circle of his arms and the way he looked at her. And that he offered her space—and friendship—when she told him that was what she needed. *For now.*

Quit analyzing everything, and just enjoy this feeling.

She let out a long breath and relaxed into him as he whirled her around the dance floor. She wasn't ready for the song—or this fairy tale night—to end.

The band played the last chords then started right into another song, this one even slower and more romantic. Mack pulled her closer, swaying to the music instead of traveling around the floor. She laid her head on his broad shoulder, closing her eyes as she inhaled the woodsy citrus scent of him.

She'd just told him she needed a friend, but she didn't have any other friends who made her heart race, and her palms sweat the way this man did.

A vibration hummed through her chest.

Mack peered down at her, a teasing grin on his face. "Is that your chest vibrating, or are you just happy to be with me?"

Dancing with him had a lot more than just her chest vibrating. She could feel the heat of him all the way to her bones and missed that warmth as she drew back. "It's my phone," she told him, pulling the device out from where she'd tucked it into the side of her bra.

Mack's eyes widened as he dipped his head closer and peered down into her cleavage. "What else you got in there? I'm kind of hungry. Any chance there's a snack?"

She was laughing with him, until she saw the name of the caller. Then panic filled her chest.

Why would Gertie be calling her this late at night unless something had happened to Izzy?

Chapter Five

Lorna tapped the answer button on her phone then plugged her opposite ear in order to better hear over the noise of the reception. "Hello. Gertie? Is everything okay?"

"Now I'm sure everything is going to be fine," the older woman assured her as Lorna was already heading off the dance floor and out of the tent. "But Izzy started fussing a bit tonight and rubbing at her ear, and then she spiked a fever, so I'm brought her over to the emergency room to have someone take a quick look at her."

"Good. You did the right thing," Lorna told her, trying to calm her racing heart and not panic. "Have they seen her yet?"

"No, I just checked her in, but I wanted to call and tell you what was happening. I'm so sorry to ruin your fun night."

"Don't worry about that." She'd known the night was just a fairy tale anyway. "I'll meet you at the hospital as soon as I can."

"What's going on? Is Izzy okay?" Mack's voice came from right behind her.

She jumped, not realizing he'd followed her outside. "I hope so. She spiked a fever, so the woman watching her took her to the hospital."

"How can I help? What do you need?"

"I need to get Max then find someone here who's sober and can drive me to the hospital." She wasn't drunk, but she'd had several seltzers and wouldn't chance getting in the car to drive.

Leni and Chevy had arranged a couple of shuttles to take people back to town after the reception. Maybe she could find one of the drivers and get him to drop her at the emergency room.

"I can do it," he said. "I only had a few sips of champagne earlier during the toasts."

"Are you sure?" She hadn't been with him the whole time, but now that she thought about it, she hadn't seen him holding a beer at all that night.

"Yes, absolutely. I'm a hundred percent sober," he said, already shepherding her back inside to the table where Max was playing a card game with Duke and Maisie's grandmother, Ruby Foster.

Lorna quickly explained the situation to Duke and Ruby, who said they'd be glad to keep Max with them and that they'd put him to bed in the ranch house if it got too late.

She turned to leave, but her shoe hit a puddle of some kind of spilled liquid, and her foot went sliding out from under her. Her arms pinwheeled before she lost her balance and hit the floor. Her dress, with its flouncy skirt, flew up as her legs splayed out.

Mack knelt next to her and flipped her dress back down, but not before she'd flashed him, and the rest of the wedding guests around them, a nice shot of her high-waisted, nude colored spanx. *So sexy.*

Maisie came hurrying toward her as Mack helped her back up. "Oh my gosh, are you okay?"

Her pride was hurt more than her butt had been, but she still imagined she'd have a bruise the next day. "Yes, I'm just not used to wearing high heels."

"Me neither. That's why I already changed out of mine and into my Chacos," Maisie said, pointing to her feet and the black, thick-soled hiking sandals that were a staple in most every woman in Colorado's closet.

"Smart," Lorna said, then told her how they were trying to get to the hospital to check on Izzy.

"I'm so sorry," Maisie said, then kicked off her sandals. "Here, trade me shoes. You can't be running into the hospital in those heels."

"Are you sure?"

"Of course, I've got another little pair of sneakers in my bag. I'm a librarian, comfy shoes and always bringing a book are my lifestyle choices."

Lorna wrenched off her heels and groaned in relief as she slipped her feet into the sandals. Then she hugged Maisie, and she and Mack hurried from the tent and toward his truck.

He got there first and pulled the door open for her, holding out his arm to help her into the cab, then he ran around the front of the truck and slid inside.

His truck smelled like leather and the woodsy citrus scent of his cologne. There was an empty water bottle in the cup holder and an orange Reese's Peanut Butter Cup wrapper on the floor, but it otherwise showed no signs that he'd just driven a day and a half, and across three states, in it.

She buckled her seatbelt then sent a quick text to Leni, telling her not to worry, but that she had to run out to check on something with Izzy and she hoped to be back later. She doubted she would go back to the reception, but didn't want her sister to worry, especially since they didn't really know anything yet.

She wished she could keep herself from worrying.

Thankfully, Mack was a good driver and was wasting no time as he flew down the highway toward town.

She should probably let it go, but something was bugging her, and she needed to know. "Hey Mack, can I ask you something?"

"Of course."

"It might be kind of personal."

He shrugged. "You can still ask."

"It's just that so many people at the wedding were drinking and partying. Is there a reason you weren't?" She was trying to keep her alarm bells from ringing. She'd already spent too much of her life with someone who had a problem with booze. "Do you have an issue with alcohol?"

He hazarded a quick glance in her direction. "Are you asking if I'm an alcoholic?"

"Maybe. I've spent too many years living with one, so yeah. I guess I'm trying to ask you that without actually asking you that."

"You never have to worry about asking me anything. I'll always tell you the truth. And no, I'm not an alcoholic. But I grew up with one, so I know the effects that can have on a person and on a family."

"So do I. Not with my parents, but with my ex."

He nodded. She knew he'd heard the story of how Lyle had taken off with his administrative assistant right after they learned she was pregnant.

"It seems to me that kids who grow up in that kind of environment tend to either follow in the footsteps of their alcoholic parent or go the opposite direction and don't drink much at all," he said, his gaze still trained on the highway. "I can enjoy an occasional cold beer with friends, but I don't drink often. And tonight, in particular, with everyone drinking and having a good time, I wanted to make sure I was sober in case Chevy or Leni needed me for something."

"That was thoughtful of you. Especially since it turned out that I was the one who needed you for something."

"I'm glad I could help. This is what friends do, right?" He reached over and took her hand, squeezed it, then let it go. "And don't worry, I'm sure Izzy is going to be just fine."

She nodded, but couldn't help the shiver that ran through her, and she rubbed at her bare arms as if to stave off the cold.

Mack pulled a faded blue and white flannel shirt from behind the seat. "Here, put this on. You already seem cold, and hospitals tend to be chilly."

She pulled the shirt on and wrapped her arms around her middle, the faded flannel soft against her skin. The fabric smelled like him, and somehow the shirt felt like a warm hug.

The drive into town only took a few minutes then a few minutes more to get to the hospital on the opposite side. Mack turned into the parking lot and found a spot close to the entrance.

She had her door open and was climbing out of the truck before he'd pulled to a complete stop. She heard him slam the truck door and the beep of the key fob, but didn't slow down. It didn't take much for his long strides to catch up to her, and he pulled the entrance door open for her then followed her to the check-in desk.

Because Woodland Hills was a small town, and she'd practically grown up there, Lorna recognized the woman at the desk. They'd gone to school together, but she'd been a few years younger.

"Hey Lorna," the woman said, already holding out two visitor passes as she pointed to a set of a double doors. "They just took Izzy back. Put this on, then you can go on through. The nurse inside will tell you what bay she's in."

"Thanks Sara," Lorna said, peeling the slick backing from the visitor sticker and slapping it to the front of the flannel shirt as she hurried toward the doors.

Another nurse sat inside, this one a young guy she didn't recognize. He wore light blue scrubs with cartoon dogs on them and smiled up at her from the desk. "Can I help you?"

"I'm looking for Isabel Williams. She's my daughter, but she was just brought in with Gertie Henderson."

"Of course. She's in that third bay, the one with the green curtain," he told her.

The emergency room section of the hospital had seven rooms, each behind a different colored curtain, as if this were a game show and there might be a new car, or a washer and dryer set, behind them instead of someone suffering with an illness or injury.

The pitiful cry of an unhappy baby came from

the direction the nurse pointed, and Lorna hurried toward it. Mack was right on her heels and drew the green curtain back to reveal a petite older woman with a cap of curly white hair standing behind it, her body swaying back and forth as she tried to soothe the fussy infant in her arms.

"I'm here," Lorna said.

At the sound of her mother's voice, Izzy lifted her head then stretched out her arms as she let loose with another heartbreaking cry. "Ma-ma."

"It's okay, baby," Lorna said, taking Izzy into her arms and starting the same rocking movement Gertie had been doing. "Mama's here." The baby's face was flushed, and her curly blond hair was damp with sweat. Lorna pressed a kiss to her forehead and that clawing panic returned at how hot her skin was. "Have you seen the doctor yet?" she asked Gertie.

The other woman shook her head. "No, we're still waiting."

Lorna tried to introduce the two, but Gertie explained she and Mack had met the summer before at the chili cook-off.

"Ma'am." Mack tipped his hat at the older woman, but his attention was focused on the baby girl in Lorna's arms. "Poor sweetheart." He stood at the entrance of the exam room, the small space already crowded with the two women and the baby. "What can I do? Do you want me to find you all some coffee? Or water? Or try to check on where the doctor is?"

Lorna nodded, and he turned and headed toward the nurse's station before she'd had a chance to tell him which of the things she wanted.

She cooed softly into Izzy's hair, still rocking her

and thankful that the baby seemed to be calming with the arrival of her mother.

Mack was back within minutes, three bottles of water in his hand. "We're next on the list, so the doctor should be here any second," he said as he passed Gertie a bottle of water. He took a moment to open the lid of one before he passed it to Lorna, whose hands were full with Izzy, and she once again, appreciated his thoughtfulness.

She took a drink, thankful for the cool water on her parched throat, then passed it back to him. He replaced the lid and had just set it on the counter when the doctor walked in.

He looked to be in his late forties with brown hair, a pleasant smile, and a pair of reading glasses perched on his head. "Hello. I'm Dr. MacFarlane," he said, picking up the clipboard the nurse had left and quickly perusing the notes. "Tell me what's going on with this little cutie?"

Gertie rattled off Izzy's symptoms, the fussiness, the rubbing at her ear, then the sudden spike of fever.

The doctor had Lorna sit on the table with Izzy on her lap, then listened to the baby's chest, tapped her tummy, and peeked into her ears and throat. "Yeah, she's got a pretty good ear infection going on. I'll have the nurse bring in some children's Motrin to treat the fever, and I'll write a script for some antibiotics. You'll want to keep up with lots of fluids and rest, and if it seems like the ear is bothering her, using a warm compress against it will help with the pain."

"So, she's going to be okay?" Mack asked the doctor, his mouth set in a tight line.

Lorna hadn't realized how worried he'd been—

he'd seemed like such a rock for her since she'd taken the call from Gertie, but now that the doctor was there, she could see the concern in his expression and hear it in his tone.

"We'll keep an eye on her here for a bit," the doctor told them. "Make sure the Motrin brings her fever down, but she should be just fine."

Lorna laid a reassuring hand on Mack's arm. "Ear infections are pretty common. Max used to get them too." She turned back to the doctor. "Thank you."

"Yes, thank you," Gertie repeated. "She was fine earlier today, so it just scared me when she spiked a fever and started fussing."

"You did the right thing by bringing her in," the doctor told them. "And like I said, we'll have you all hang around for an hour or so, just to make sure we get the fever down. I'll go get started on the prescription and the nurse will be in shortly."

"That's a relief," Gertie said, sagging into the chair after the doctor left. "I would have felt terrible if something had happened to our sweet girl."

Lorna gave her a one-armed hug. "Thank you so much for calling me and for everything. Are you doing okay? You must be tired."

"I'm fine. Although, it's been a while since I've stayed up past nine."

"I can run Miss Gertie home," Mack offered. "Then I can come back and get you. It'll probably take me less than ten minutes."

Lorna considered his offer. "Honestly, if Gertie is okay staying with me, I'd rather have you run back out to the ranch and get Max. I know Duke offered to let him spend the night, but I'd rather have him home and just let them enjoy the wedding and not have to worry about him."

"Yeah, sure. I can absolutely do that."

Gertie nodded. "I'm happy to stay and drive you home. Plus, I've got Izzy's car seat in my car."

"There's a booster seat for Max in my car, which is still parked at the ranch. I'll give you my keys and you can take my car." Lorna looked around the exam room. "Actually, I just realized I don't have my purse. I think I left it in the master bedroom where Leni was getting dressed. Can you grab it too? It's light pink, and I've got a glittery pink and white tote bag, but I can grab that tomorrow if you can't find it."

Mack nodded. "So, pink purse and glittery pink bag. I can only hope your car is a hot pink minivan."

"I wish." She grinned, trying to imagine the tough cowboy driving a pink van. "You can move the booster into your truck, if you'd rather. It just buckles in."

"I'll probably move the seat, just so I'll have my truck to get home, but my man card is secure enough that I can carry your purse, glitter and all. Is there anything else you need me to do?"

"Just tell Duke and Ruby thank you for watching Max. I'll text Leni what's going on, but if she and Chevy haven't left yet, tell them again that I'm sorry I'm missing the end of the reception."

"Will do. And I'm sure they'll understand." He stepped forward and pulled her and the baby in her arms to him in a gentle hug. "I'm real glad Izzy is going to be okay. Not embarrassed to admit she had me scared there for a minute." He dipped his head and pressed a kiss to the top of the baby's head then flashed Lorna a grin before letting them both go. "Text me if you need anything else."

He pulled the curtain closed behind him, and Lorna looked at Gertie as the sound of his boot heels faded.

The older woman fanned her face. "I think Izzy's fever might be catching, because it's suddenly very warm in here."

Lorna laughed. "Stop."

Gertie gave her a side eye. "That is one handsome man. And thoughtful too. Now, I'm even more sorry we interrupted your night. Looks like you might have been having wedding cake *and* a cowboy for dessert."

"We're just friends," Lorna told her, although she had a hard time meeting Gertie's eye when she said it.

"Has anyone told him that?"

Chapter Six

THIRTY MINUTES LATER, after assuring Duke and Ruby that Izzy was going to be okay and collecting all the glittery bags and one wired six-year-old who was hyped up on wedding cake and soda, Mack walked into Lorna's yellow house at the end of Aspen Grove Lane.

The spacious two-story had been Lorna and Leni's home growing up. Their mother had bought the house and moved the three of them to Woodland Hills after their father had walked out on them.

He knew Lorna and Max had moved back into the house with her mom after that jackass, Lyle, had taken off with his secretary and left his family behind. But then, during the middle of Lorna's pregnancy, her mom remarried and moved to Florida with her new husband and had left Lorna the house for her and the kids.

The interior was spacious, an open concept with a big living room in the front and a sunny kitchen in the back. A flight of stairs in between led up to the four bedrooms on the second floor. A laundry room, office and small family room sat off to the side of the kitchen, and a large pergola-covered patio led into a huge backyard with a view of the mountains and a creek that ran behind the house.

Lorna's decorating style tended to be a lot of blues, whites, and grays intermixed with jam-packed bookcases, tons of throw pillows, a few plants, and masses of kid paraphernalia. The overstuffed couch had two baskets of unfolded laundry stacked in one corner, and toys littered the floor. The house smelled like vanilla candles with a hint of baby powder.

And Mack loved it.

He'd grown up in crappy apartments and trailer parks, and everything he'd owned fit into the two large duffle bags he was allowed to move from one shitty place to the next. He'd never had a yard to play in or shelves filled with books.

Lorna had created a home for her children here. Sure, it was messy, with toys scattered everywhere and dishes stacked in the sink, but he would bet there was food in the cupboards and milk in the refrigerator that hadn't been expired for weeks.

"All right, bud, time for bed," he told Max.

Lorna had already texted him detailed instructions on where to find pajamas for Max, his two favorite books, and to make sure he brushed his teeth before going to bed.

The little boy groaned—an exaggerated sound accompanied by a sigh too heavy for a six-year-old. "*Do I have to?* I'm not even tired. Can't we do something fun?"

"We could spend a little time cleaning up in here. Make it a surprise for your mom?"

Max frowned. "Do you even know what fun means? Cleaning up is *not* fun."

"It can be." He slid two of the empty toy bins into the center of the room. "Bet I can fill this bin with toys faster than you can fill that one. I'll time us and see who can get more in three minutes?"

Max offered him a cautious side eye then grinned. "Do bigger toys count for two points or one?"

Mack loved a good negotiation. "Two, but only if they're twice as big as a smaller one you put in. And you can count three points if you toss one and land it in the bin, but only if it's a stuffed animal and nothing that can break."

The boy's eyes widened then he leaned down, picked up a stuffed giraffe and chucked it across the room. It hit the side of one of the bins then dropped in. "I'm winning," he crowed then raced around the room, ignoring the other toys as he flung every stuffed animal he could find toward his bin.

Mack focused on all the other toys, sweeping them into his arms and depositing them into the tubs. It only took a few minutes to clear the floor, and he declared Max the winner without even counting. "Now, let's tackle these baskets of laundry."

"Aww." Max blew a raspberry. "Do all your games include cleaning?"

He laughed. "Tonight they do. Besides, cleaning up can be fun."

"You're weird."

He chuckled again. "Listen, buddy, your sister isn't feeling well, and your mom is my friend, so I want to help her. Then when she comes home, she can focus on you and Izzy, and she won't have to worry about this other stuff."

Max let out another heaving sigh. "*Ohhhhh*-kay, I'll help." He picked a small blue washcloth out of the basket and grinned slyly as he held it up. "How many points do I get for folding this?"

It only took about ten minutes for them to fold the clothes, then Max showed him where everything went, so they got it all put away as well. Mack pulled out the vacuum, promising to read Max three books if he got his pajamas on and brushed his teeth while he swept the floors.

Mack had vacuumed the living room carpet, the throw rugs, and the hardwood floors and was putting the machine back into the closet when Max raced down the stairs, wearing mismatched pajamas and carrying three books. He crouched down to the boy's level. "Did you brush your teeth really well?"

Max nodded then blew a minty breath in his face.

Three books, two stories, one hug, and a glass of water later, Mack finally got the little boy to bed. Lorna texted to say the nurse had just brought the discharge papers, so he figured he'd have time to tackle the dishes in the sink before they got home.

He'd loaded the dishwasher, washed the pans, lit one of her fancy-smelling candles, and had just finished wiping down the stove and counters when Lorna walked through the door, the car seat looped over her arm with a sleeping Izzy tucked inside.

"How's she doing?" he asked quietly, taking the car seat from her and gently setting it on the table.

"Better. The Motrin brought her fever down, and she stopped fussing." Lorna was still wearing his blue flannel shirt, and the sight of her wrapped up in it made him happy.

Her eyes went wide as she looked around the house, and then she flung her arms around Gertie as the older woman walked into the kitchen. "Wow, thank you, Gertie. The house looks amazing. You picked up the toys and folded that dang laundry I've been meaning to get to. And you cleaned the kitchen *and* ran the vacuum. You didn't have to do all this."

"I didn't," Gertie told her. "I didn't do *any* of it." She glanced over at Mack, who was leaning his hip against the counter and shaking his head at her as if he didn't need the credit. "But I can guess who did."

Lorna turned to Mack, her expression one of surprise. "You did all this? The laundry? The vacuuming? The kitchen?"

He shrugged. "Max helped. He showed me where to put the laundry away, and some of his directions seemed questionable, so if you're missing something, I'd asked him where to find it." He grinned at his joke then teasingly held his arms out in case she wanted to give him the same kind of hug she'd given Gertie.

But she didn't run over and throw her arms around him. Instead, she shifted her weight to one foot and frowned. "But why?"

Gertie cleared her throat. "Ahem. I think what she meant to say was *thank you.*"

Mack shook his head. "I didn't do it for the thanks," he said, then offered her a teasing grin. "Although I'm a little disappointed to not get one of those big hugs…"

"Then why?" she asked again, her expression still wary.

"Because I wanted to help. Izzy was sick and you were worried, and I felt bad that you missed the end of the reception. And because this is what a friend would do."

Her expression softened. "Thank you." Her voice came out as a whisper. "I guess I'm just not used to being offered help."

"Without strings being attached?" he wanted to ask. But kept his mouth shut.

"Well, I think it was awful sweet of you," Gertie said. "And I'll take this kind of help any day. In fact, if you're free tomorrow, you can come over to my house and run the sweeper, and I've got some dusting to do, and the lawn could use a mow. And if you get hot, you can feel free to take your shirt off. I won't mind a bit." She winked at Mack and offered him a coy, teasing grin.

He laughed. "I'd be happy to help you, Miss Gertie. Any time. But I'm keeping my shirt on."

Gertie shrugged. "Let's keep the option open. I'm a good tipper."

Lorna laughed and playfully swatted at the older woman. "Miss Gertie, you are incorrigible."

"I know." Gertie winked again then unbuckled and carefully lifted Izzy out of her car seat. "I'll take this little cutie upstairs and put her to bed."

"Is there anything else I can do to help?" Mack asked as Gertie disappeared up the stairs.

Lorna shook her head. "No. Thank you. You've already done so much. I still can't believe you folded and put away all that laundry. It's been sitting there for a week." She covered her face with her hands. "I'm just thankful it hadn't been a basket of *my* socks and undies. I think I would have died if I'd come home to find you'd folded my granny panties then put them away in my way-too-boring underwear drawer."

He blinked, really wanting to say something about how he could be the judge of how boring her undies drawer was, but he was trying to stay in the friend zone, so he ignored her comment and kept his reply light. "Like I said, Max helped."

She huffed out a laugh. "Which also seems like a miracle. I don't know how you did all this *and* still got him to bed."

"I wasn't trying to also take care of an infant and run a business and cook three meals a day."

"True. But I still appreciate it." She covered her mouth as a yawn escaped.

"Guess I'd better get back to the ranch and see if they need any help cleaning up after the reception."

"Wow, you're on a real roll tonight with helping people pick things up."

He shrugged. "I don't mind helping. It might sound dumb, but I wished for a real family for so long, and now that I have one, it feels good to be part of something. And I know they've only been my family for a minute, but I would do anything for them."

"That doesn't sound dumb at all," she told him. "Family is everything."

He walked to the door but paused just inside it. "Keep me posted on how Izzy's doing, and text me if you need anything. I mean it."

"Hey, you forgot this." She walked across the room and into his arms.

He held her against him, the scent of her shampoo filling the air around him. The bobby pins had come loose in a few places, and pieces of her hair fell in soft ringlets against the bare skin of her neck.

And it was taking everything in him not to lift a lock of it and sift it between his fingers, then press his lips to the creamy length of her neck.

"Thanks for everything," she said into his chest. "You were a total rock for me tonight. And I feel like I owe you more than a hug for loading my dishwasher and vacuuming the floor."

He jostled her against him, lowering his voice as he leaned closer to her ear. "What kind of *more* did you have in mind?"

She grinned coyly up at him. "I'm thinking about offering you my first-born son. He's a bit of a talker but he's pretty skilled at checkers."

He laughed. "I'm already taking over Chevy's old room at the ranch. Duke might frown on me bringing in a roommate already. Although he does love a good game of checkers."

"Max is your guy then. He's a great player if you don't mind him making up his own rules and changing them midway through the match."

"Sounds like my kind of game, but still..." He lifted one shoulder as he smiled down at her. "Maybe you'd better hold on to him for a while."

"Yeah, I think I will. Despite his questionable gaming skills, he's still pretty dang cute and one heck of a hugger."

Speaking of being cute and a good hugger. Lorna hadn't pulled away from him and he relished the feel of her encircled in his arms, her lush body snug against his, fitting perfectly to him as if they were the last two pieces of a puzzle.

And he wasn't ready for her to pull away. He hadn't realized how much he'd missed her—her easy laugh, her clever wit, her profound love for her children.

He reached up, cupped her cheek in his palm as he peered into her eyes, all traces of teasing gone. "I meant what I said about family and what it means to me. And now that your sister and my brother are married, that makes you and me—and Max and Izzy—family too. So, whatever you need, I got you."

He leaned down to press a kiss to her cheek. He'd meant it to be a friendly one—yeah, right, if he were honest with himself, he'd admit that he just wanted his lips on her, anywhere—but as his face neared hers, she turned just the slightest and the side of his lips caught the edge of hers.

Chapter Seven

LORNA'S BREATH CAUGHT at the brush of Mack's lips against the corner of her mouth.

It had been seven years since she'd kissed anyone other than Lyle—and she couldn't remember ever feeling this way with him. Ever feeling this way with *anyone*.

Heart pounding, stomach churning, heat rushing through her body as sweat formed in the small of her back—she was terrified and excited at the same time, exhilarated while also feeling a bit like she might throw up.

And it was wonderful.

It lasted only a second—surely not long enough for those millions of emotions and sensations to run through her—and no way could it have been long enough for her to already miss the feeling…but she did.

He pulled back, but not *away*, the barest space between his lips and her skin. She couldn't move, could barely breathe, anticipation coursing through her as she waited to see if he would kiss her again.

What if he does? Do I want him to kiss me again?
Will I die if he doesn't?
Or if he does?

She could still feel the barest traces of his lips against her skin. His breath caressed her cheek as time seemed to stand still.

Was he waiting for a sign from her? Waiting for her to give him any kind of indication that she wanted more.

She'd already told him she wanted to be friends. She was a mess…he'd witnessed, *and cleaned up*, just a small slice of the chaos of her life. She didn't have time—or hell, even the energy—for one more thing in her life. Max and Izzy and running a business and a house took everything from her.

So, why hadn't she pulled away?

She wasn't sure who moved. It could have been him…or her…or both at the same moment. All she knew—all she *felt*—was the brush of his lips against hers, a soft graze, this time fully against her mouth, not just the corner.

A tiny gasp escaped her, a small shuddering breath before his lips pressed to hers, capturing the rest of her exhale, taking in her breath as if it were his own.

She melted into him, her bones dissolving as his arms tightened around her, pulling her closer to him and keeping her from sinking into the floor.

"I got Izzy down and thought I'd make us a cup of tea," Gertie's voice came from the stairwell.

Lorna pulled back. Fast. Stepping back as if his body were on fire.

"Oops, sorry," Gertie said, stepping into the living room, seeing them then turning to head into the kitchen. "Didn't mean to interrupt. Pretend I'm not even here."

Mack offered her a sheepish grin. "I guess I should go. Be sure to text me about how Izzy's doing tomorrow. Good night, Lorna." He retrieved his cowboy hat from the side table and gave her a nod before putting it on his head and slipping out the door.

She touched her fingers to her lips—surprised to feel the tremble in them—as she watched him amble across the grass to where his pickup was parked.

Wrapping her arms around her middle, the scent of him still surrounding her, she felt something inside her shift. An ache she'd buried a long time ago resurfacing. And she wasn't sure if she wanted to embrace it or push it back down again.

The reception had ended, and the guests were gone by the time Mack got back to the ranch. Ford, Elizabeth, Dodge, Maisie, and a few members of the band were the only ones left when Mack walked into the large white tent.

Two golden retrievers, one russet and one yellow, came loping toward him, their furry butts wagging with excitement. Dixie, the red one, belonged to Ford, and Murphy, the English Cream, was Chevy's dog. Mack crouched down to receive the puppy love, wanting to believe that the dogs remembered him. But the goldens seemed to love everyone.

"Hey, how's Izzy doing?" Elizabeth asked, as the two couples, who were stacking chairs and packaging leftover food stopped what they were doing and crossed to him.

"Is Lorna okay?" Maisie asked.

"Yeah, they're all good," Mack told them. "The doctor gave Izzy some antibiotics for the ear infection, but they're home now. The kids were asleep, and Miss Gertie was still there when I left."

"That's good," Ford said, as Dixie circled his legs then dropped at his feet.

"Where's Moose?" Mack asked Dodge, referring to his giant black Bernese Mountain dog.

"We left him at Maisie's," Dodge said.

Maisie laughed. "But we promised to bring him some brisket." She pointed to the takeaway aluminum tubs stacked on one of the tables. "Which shouldn't be a problem. We've got enough food left to stock Duke's fridge and for each of us to take some home."

"It was so good, I'm surprised there was any left." Mack gestured at the remaining tables and chairs. "Can I help?"

"You bet," Ford told him. "The girls are gonna finish packing up the centerpieces and pulling the tablecloths, what's left of the band is dismantling the dance floor, and we're stacking all the tables and chairs." He pointed to an open trailer that had been backed up to the side of the tent. "The rental company is coming in the morning to pick them up and take down the tent. We figured we'd get it all torn down now since we've got cattle to take care of in the morning."

"Sounds good," Mack said, feeling glad they had asked him to help versus sending him on up to the house as he headed for the nearest table and chairs.

The sun was barely up the next morning when, freshly showered and dressed, Mack walked into the kitchen to find Duke already at the stove, scrambling chunks of leftover brisket into a skillet of fluffy yellow eggs.

The scent of strong coffee wafted toward him, and Duke nodded to the cupboard. "Mornin' son. You'd better grab you a mug and get some of that pot of coffee before your brothers get here."

The front door opened a few seconds later, and Ford and Dodge came in together, the cool morning air whooshing in with them as they stopped to brush off their boots and hang their cowboy hats and gray Carhartt jackets on pegs running down the wall inside the door.

Their two dogs and Chevy's raced in behind them, tails wagging at top speed as they ran into the kitchen to greet Duke and Mack, probably hoping to get tastes of the barbequed meat filling the air with its delicious scent.

Mack held the pot up and filled his brother's mugs as Duke pulled a pan of flaky buttermilk biscuits out of the oven. He'd tasted Duke's biscuits when he'd been here before, and his stomach growled for one… or six.

"Grab a plate and dig in," Duke commanded. "These biscuits are best hot with butter melting into them."

Mack didn't have to be told twice. He grabbed a couple of plates and passed them to Ford and Dodge, hanging back as the youngest and newest Lassiter brother before filling his plate and taking a place at the large kitchen table.

Duke said grace before passing around the pitcher of orange juice and large bowls filled with chunked cantaloupe and wedges of watermelon.

The first bite of fluffy eggs mixed with the smokey brisket and sharp cheddar cheese was like a flavor explosion in his mouth. "So good," he told Duke in between bites. "Anyone hear if Chevy and Leni got off okay?"

Dodge smirked. "It was their wedding night. I think we can be fairly certain they got off…multiple times."

Ford threw a chunk of biscuit at his brother. It fell to the floor and the three dogs raced to grab it. "Not while I'm eating."

"Chevy texted me earlier and said they were headed to DIA," Duke told them, ignoring Ford and Dodge's comments as he tossed more biscuit to the two dogs who'd missed the first chunk. "Their plane leaves in about an hour."

"I'm still having a hard time imagining Chevy sitting on the beach in Hawaii," Dodge said, reaching for another wedge of melon.

Ford grinned. "I'm having a hard time imagining him in a pair of flip flops. I can just see him walking out onto the sand in his swim trunks, cowboy hat and boots."

The men laughed together, but Mack knew they were all happy that Chevy and Leni had found their way back to each other after years apart.

"I appreciate you all lending me his room," Mack said as he buttered his third biscuit.

"It's your room now, son," Duke told him. "He cleaned it out last week for you and either moved his stuff to the cabin or stored it in the bunkhouse."

"Still hard to believe Chevy and Leni are going to spend the whole summer in that tiny hunting cabin," Dodge said.

Ford huffed. "Sounds like paradise to me. They've got the lake and nobody around to bother them." He was the most introverted of the bunch.

"They're newlyweds," Duke said as if that explained everything. "And it's only for a few months until their house is built."

The newly married couple had drawn up plans and commissioned a contractor to build their dream house in the mountains on the Lassiter property. Construction had started a few weeks ago, and they hoped to have it finished and ready to move into by the fall.

"Don't sweat it," Dodge said. "The room is yours now. For as long as you want it."

Ford dumped the last of the eggs onto his plate. "But so are the bulk of Chevy's chores while he's gone."

Mack nodded. "I'm happy to do them. I still feel a little guilty that I didn't get back here sooner. I swear I didn't know I'd be gone that long when I agreed to go back to Texas to help my old foreman."

Duke shook his head. "Don't give it another thought. That wasn't your fault. You were where you needed to be at the time, and I know they appreciated the extra help."

"I appreciate you saying so, but I've already told them I'm done with Texas." Colorado and this ranch were where he wanted his home to be now. The first real home he'd ever had. "I'm back for good this time, and the only place I'm planning to work is for this ranch."

Ford stuffed the last of a biscuit into his mouth and spoke around it as he chewed. "Then cowboy up, boys. Daylight's burning, and we've got plenty of work to do."

The late spring sun had already heated the day up by midmorning, and the barn was warm as Mack mucked out the stalls and laid fresh straw for the horses. He'd taken his shirt off earlier, tossing it over the gate of the nearest corral, and he rolled his shoulders as he stopped to take a sip of water from a bottle he'd brought out to the barn.

The cool water felt good on his dry throat, and he took off his hat and splashed a little on his head before pushing his hair back and cramming his straw cowboy hat back on. He'd just picked up the pitchfork to start the next stall when he heard one side of the barn door swing open.

"Gertie's gonna be mad she missed out on seeing you working without your shirt on," a voice called from behind him.

A grin was already creasing his face as he turned to face Lorna. She looked different from the night before, more like the way he was used to seeing her in a pair of black yoga pants, sneakers, and a hot pink

V-neck T-shirt, but still gorgeous with her thick curly blond hair gathered and pulled into a messy knot on top of her head. "Hey there. You're the best thing I've seen all day."

Lorna glanced into the wheelbarrow of muck he'd been cleaning from the stall. "That would be more of a compliment if I couldn't see my competition. Doesn't seem like I've got too much in the way of opposition."

He laughed. "What are you doing here? Not that I'm not glad to see you."

"Maisie was coming out to see Dodge, so I grabbed a ride with her to get the rest of my stuff and pick up my van." Her eyes roamed over his chest as he leaned on the pitchfork. "Dang. Did you have to pay for all those muscles or were you just born that way?"

He grinned as he reached for his shirt, giving her a quick flex of his bicep in the process. "I earned every one of them."

"You don't have to wear your shirt on my account. Especially since it is pretty warm in here."

"Is that why your cheeks are so flushed?"

"I don't know what you're talking about." She pressed her fingers to her face, her cheeks going even more pink. "Anyway, Duke told me you were out here, so I wanted to pop in to tell you Max is dying to get started on that Lego set, but he's under the impression that you are planning to build it with him, so he doesn't want to do any of it without you."

Mack chuckled, touched that the boy would want to wait for him. "Yeah, I would love to help him build it. Just let me know when's a good time."

"How about later this afternoon? I'm making

spaghetti and wanted to invite you for supper anyway as a thank you for all your help last night."

"No thanks necessary. I was happy to do it. But I have never turned down a plate of spaghetti—it's one of my top three favorite meals—so I'll be there."

"Four o'clock?"

"Works for me. Can I bring anything?"

"Just your LEGO building skills, your appetite…" Her lips curved into a coy grin. "And those muscles."

Chapter Eight

NO MATTER HOW many times she told herself to stop doing it, Lorna couldn't help flirting with Mack Lassiter. It was so fun to see his neck go pink when she played with him or to watch the grin teasing the corners of his lips.

Even though she'd told him he didn't have to bring anything, he still showed up with a bottle of wine and a carton of vanilla ice cream—two of her favorite things. And both would go with the surprise she had for him after supper.

She'd set up a folding table in the small family room off the kitchen and taped the instructions for building the pirate ship on the wall next to it. From past Lego sets, they'd learned to divide out like pieces into small containers before they started, and she and Max had spent an hour before Mack got there prepping for the build.

"Wow, it smells amazing in here," Mack had said when he'd walked in the door and inhaled the scents of tomato sauce and garlic filling the house.

She'd taken advantage of Izzy's afternoon nap and had got the table set and the garlic bread buttered and wrapped in foil. She'd put together a salad and made the spaghetti sauce then put the salad in the fridge and the sauce in a crockpot so all she'd have to do is boil the pasta and pop the bread in the oven when they were ready to eat.

Mack had been super impressed with their prep work and the Lego building command central they'd created, and over the last twenty minutes, they'd put together the base of the ship and were starting on the sails.

Lorna spent most of her time trying to keep the small pieces away from Izzy's eager fingers and was relieved when the baby arched her back and kicked her legs to be let down. But she was quite surprised when the baby crawled across the floor and pulled herself up Mack's leg then lifted her arms toward him. She was even more shocked to watch the cowboy absently lift her and a stuffed toy from the floor up into his lap, tuck her into the crook of his shoulder, all while still fiddling with trying to fit two Lego pieces together.

Izzy usually shied away from men, with the exception of the Lassiter men, Chevy and Duke in particular. Lorna assumed it was because one was around all the time *and* her new uncle and because of the other one's similarity to Santa Claus.

But Mack hadn't been around for months. It was true that he'd held her a lot when she was an infant—Lorna remembered the first day she'd met Mack and how surprised she'd been when he took a turn carrying Izzy strapped to his chest for hours while they dished up samples at the annual chili cook off.

He'd always been comfortable around the baby and Max. A sudden thought occurred to her.

"Izzy doesn't usually take to people like she does to you," Lorna told him. "And most men aren't eager to hold a baby, but you just scooped her right up."

He leveled her with one of his serious stares. "I think I've mentioned before that I am *not* like most men."

"Yes, you have. But it makes me wonder..." She looked down as she ran her finger along a small scratch in the table before raising her eyes to meet his gaze again. "Do you already have kids?"

He shook his head but kept his gaze trained on hers. "No. I don't. But for a while, when I was younger, I was around little kids quite a bit."

"How so?"

"When I was around ten or eleven, we lived in this crummy little apartment building in a small town in Texas. Our neighbors across the hall were this nice young couple who had four kids, all younger than me, including a baby. The woman—her name was Anna Maria—" He smiled fondly when he said her name. "I think she must have noticed that my mom was gone a lot and tended to leave me alone for days or weeks at a time, and she sort of took me under her wing."

Lorna noticed how he just blithely mentioned that his mother left a ten-year-old boy alone in an apartment for weeks at a time, and her heart broke for the boy he'd been.

"She started out asking if I could help her watch the kids while she went to the basement to change the laundry or to run a quick errand," Mack continued.

"Then she'd end up inviting me to stay for dinner, and most nights sent leftovers home with me, so I'd have something to eat for lunch the next day."

"Wow. That was kind of her."

"She was one of the kindest people I've ever known. But don't be mistaken." He flashed her a good-natured grin. "She made me work for it too. But I never minded. It made me feel less like a charity case to eat with their family if I'd spent the afternoon watching the kids or helping fold clothes or doing odd little chores for her. Dante, her husband, gave me some basic tools and taught me how to fix small things around the apartment like changing lightbulbs and how to stop a leak in the sink. And Anna-Maria taught me how to shop for cheap ingredients and how to cook simple meals so I could feed myself and not starve when my mom took off again. She taught me how to do my own laundry and how to make homemade tortillas and chocolate chip cookies. I don't think my mom ever baked a cookie in her life."

Hearing that made Lorna thankful for that sweet mom who took on another woman's child, and felt even more convinced Mack would appreciate the surprise she'd made for him.

"The year we lived in that apartment building was probably the happiest one of my childhood. Even though my mom was gone a lot, and my dad had already taken off by then, I still got to experience what it felt like to be part of a family. To have someone happy to see me when I got home from school and to ask about my day or praise me for a good grade. And her kids were like the siblings I'd always wished for. Every time one of them asked me to do a puzzle or play *Crazy Eights* or *Go Fish* or watch a cartoon with them, I always said yes. And I never cared about changing diapers or taking out the trash or washing dishes, as long as I got to be with them."

"They sound great. Do you still keep in touch?"

He shook his head. "Nah. My mom met some guy, and we moved to another town, and I never saw them again. But I never forgot the impact they had on my life."

"Thank you for sharing that story with me," she told him, her tone as solemn as the occasion called for. They stared at each other, both seemingly thinking about that ten-year-old boy. His story had taught her something about him. And it touched her that he'd trusted her with something so personal from his past.

"I like to play *Crazy Eights*," Max said, picking up two white Lego pieces and sticking them together. "And you can watch cartoons with me whenever you want. Have you ever seen *Bluey*? It's a show about a Blue-Heeler puppy, and she's six, like me. And she gets into trouble sometimes."

"Also like you," Lorna said, grinning at her son and the way he so effortlessly lightened the conversation.

"I have not seen it," Mack told him. "But I do like Blue-Heelers, and I'd be glad to watch it sometime with you."

"How about right now?" Max flashed his mom an innocent grin.

"How about we focus on the pirate ship for right now," she said. "And maybe we can watch an episode after supper."

"Ohh-kay," he sighed, then turned to Mack. "Will

you stay and watch one show with me? Just one. Or maybe two. They're really funny."

Mack laughed. "Sure, bud. If it's okay with your mom, I'll commit to at least one."

Lorna shrugged. "Who am I to stand in the way of a new Bluey convert? But speaking of supper, it's after five, so I'd better get the noodles going or we'll never eat."

Izzy seemed content in Mack's lap, so Lorna slipped away to the kitchen to start the pasta and get the bread into the oven.

Mack was a decent man, thoughtful and kind, and it made her happy for her son to spend time with him. But they'd spent time together before and then Mack had left for months. She was in dangerous territory here, letting herself, and her little family, get close to another man. She sure as hell didn't want her boy to have to go through the heartbreak of another guy walking out of their lives.

When she had everything ready and the food on the table, she headed back toward the family room but stopped to listen to the conversation happening between Mack and her son.

"I can't believe how quickly you put that part together," Mack was saying. "You're really smart, Max."

"No, I'm not. I'm dumb," Max answered way too matter-of-factly.

"What? Why would you say that?"

"Because that's what my daddy used to say," Max said, and a piece of Lorna's heart tore in two. "He always called me a little dummy."

"Well, he's wrong." She could hear the shock in Mack's tone.

"I know I'm not smart, I get my letters mixed up a lot. That's why I have trouble reading. But I don't mind being called dumb. He said my mama was a dummy too, and so that makes me just like her, and she's awesome."

"Max, I want you to listen to me," Mack told him, his voice taking on a serious tone. "Neither you nor your mother are dummies. In fact, you are both *very* smart. Your mom runs her own business and has to keep track of a lot of things at the coffee shop and still take care of you and your sister. And it takes someone with a lot of skill and smarts to be able to build this pirate ship. You're *not* dumb. You're a very bright kid, and I don't want you to ever let anyone tell you different or make you feel like you're dumb. That is simply *not* true."

"Okay," Max said, but so quietly, Lorna could barely hear him.

"Supper's ready," Lorna said, forcing a smile as she walked into the family room. "Max, go wash your hands and get sat up to the table."

The boy set the pieces down that he was working on and raced toward the ground floor bathroom, calling over his shoulder as he ran. "I'm having two slices of garlic bread tonight."

"I heard what you said," Lorna told Mack as she lifted the baby off his lap. "Thank you for that."

"I meant it," Mack told her, then lowered his voice. "And if I ever meet your ex, there's a strong chance I'll punch him in the throat."

"I understand the sentiment."

"How could anyone think Max is dumb? I'm amazed at the way he's been able to put this Lego thing together. Half the time, I'm still trying to figure out the instructions, and he's already got the next part built."

"He was diagnosed with dyslexia earlier this year. His kindergarten teacher recognized the signs, and she's been a great help in getting us resources and educating us on how to manage it."

"Oh wow. I never would have guessed."

"No, it's not something you can see. And sometimes kids go undiagnosed for years, so we're super thankful for Max's teacher and all the support we've received from her and the school."

"I get the first helping of *pasketti*," Max said, bursting from the bathroom, his hands still dripping water, as he raced toward the table. He pulled out the chair next to him. "Mack, you sit by me."

"Thanks bud," Mack said, ducking into the bathroom. "I gotta wash my hands, too. Don't eat all the garlic bread without me."

Yeah, Mack Lassiter was a good guy. A decent man, and just what she'd said she wanted, a good friend to her *and* her son.

So why was she checking out his butt when he walked down the hall in front of her and feeling a little jealous that Izzy was the only one who got to sit in his lap?

Chapter Nine

"That was delicious," Mack said as he pushed away from the table. "Best spaghetti I've had in years."

"You must have liked it—you ate two bowls full," Max said, slurping a noodle into his mouth.

"I'm glad you enjoyed it," Lorna said. "The sauce was my grandmother's recipe."

"Well, give her my compliments," he said.

A look of sadness washed over her face. "I wish I could, but we lost her right after I got pregnant with Izzy. I'm sad she never got to meet her great granddaughter. But she adored Max."

"Who wouldn't?" Mack said, ruffling the boy's hair. "Were you close to her?"

"Oh yeah. Leni and I both were. She was an amazing woman. She's the one who gave me the building for the coffee shop. It used to be a little flower shop that she and my grandpa ran, then she rented it out to a real estate agency after he died, and she couldn't manage it on her own anymore. I had told her my ideas of opening a coffee shop someday, and she left me the building and a little money to get it up and running."

"That was quite a gift."

"You have no idea." She wet a napkin in her water and wiped spaghetti sauce from Izzy's cheeks. "Starting that shop saved me. It gave me something positive to focus on after Lyle left, and a way to support myself and my family. We'd moved in with my mom and she helped with the kids while I worked around the clock ordering inventory, researching how to run a business, scouring thrift stores for tables and chairs, and painting and decorating the shop."

"You did an amazing job."

"Thank you. I appreciate you saying that. I'm really proud of it and what I've accomplished, basically all on my own. I worked really hard to stretch every dollar my grandmother left me, and I applied for and received a couple of small business grants. I also consciously try hard to be innovative and to help other women as well. Like, the majority of my baked goods are made by a couple of single moms, one does the pies and pastries and the other does the sandwiches and egg bites. I sell them on a consignment basis, so I can offer food, but don't have to pay for groceries or keep inventory or do any baking."

"That's really clever. I was just telling Max earlier how smart you are." Mack liked listening to her share about her accomplishments and really liked the pride he saw as she pushed her shoulders back when she told him about helping other women in the community. "I find smart to be super sexy."

She barked out a laugh as her cheeks glowed pink.

"Yeah, that's what I usually hear when I start babbling about baked goods, paint colors, and small business grants."

"If you're trying to seduce me with your business skills acumen..." He offered her one of his rakish grins. "It's working."

She laughed again, and he loved that he was bringing that happiness to her face.

"What does 'sexy' mean?" Max asked as he worked to wrangle one of his last noodles onto his fork.

Mack glanced at Lorna, who was trying to hold back a grin. "Um, well, it just means something like nice looking and well put-together."

The boy nodded in understanding. "Yeah, like my new pirate ship. It's super sexy."

"Yep. Sure is, bud." He chuckled as Lorna's phone buzzed on the counter behind them. "Saved by the bell," he whispered as she stood to grab it.

"It's one of my employees," she said before tapping the screen to answer it. "Hello, this is Lorna." She pressed her finger in her opposite ear and moved into the front room to be able to hear better.

Mack cleared the table as she talked, rinsing the plates and silverware in the sink before stacking them in the dishwasher. He was impressed that Max got up to help him, and he had the boy wrap the remaining bread in foil and show him where to find a dish for the leftover spaghetti.

He could tell the phone call wasn't a good one just by the comments Lorna was making and the concerned furrow in her brow. He'd just finished washing the last pan when she came back into the kitchen.

"Everything okay?" he asked as he wrung out the washcloth to wipe off the table.

"Not really," she said, frowning as she shoved her phone into her pocket. "One of my employees was playing hockey with her brothers this morning and broke her arm. The doctor told her she can't work for at least the next week."

"Oh, dang."

"Dang is right. I could normally manage this by asking Leni to pitch in, but since she's lounging on a beach somewhere in Hawaii right now, I'm in trouble." She took the washcloth from him and cleaned off the table, scrubbing at a spot of dried spaghetti sauce.

"I can help."

Her head popped up as she gaped at him. "You? That's sweet, but have you ever worked in a coffee shop before? Do you know how to make a caramel macchiato or a java Frappuccino?"

"I don't even know what a caramel macchiato is. But I worked in plenty of fast-food joints when I was in high school, so I know how to run a register and bus tables and serve food. I could do all that while you make the fancy coffee-java-caramel-whatever-the-heck bougie beverages you sell."

"Mack, I appreciate the offer, but you've only been home for one day and you've already helped me out so much. Thanks for cleaning the kitchen, by the way. You didn't have to do that."

"It was no big deal," he told her. "And the least I could do after you made that great meal."

Her shoulders sank as she stared at him. "It *is*

a big deal. I was married for five years, and I can't remember *one* time that my husband even carried his plate to the sink, let alone put it in the dishwasher or ever washed a pan."

"Then he wasn't a very good husband," Mack mumbled, not quite under his breath.

"No, he was not," she agreed. "So, I learned to get pretty adept at handling things on my own. And I'm not very good at asking for help."

"You're *not* asking. I'm offering. And that's what friends do. They help each other when they're in trouble." Speaking of helping, he just remembered telling Ford that morning that he could count on him to help at the ranch.

He'd just have to find a way to manage both.

Because Lorna needed him, and something in him, something that was part protective, part compassionate, and partly because he was so enamored with this woman, was compelled to do whatever he could to help her.

She stared at him, holding him in the gaze of her gorgeous gray-blue eyes, which reminded him of the summer sky, then blinked her long eyelashes and let out a relenting sigh. "Fine. You can help me. But just until I find someone else. And the shop opens early, so you would have to be there by seven."

He grinned. "Yes, chef." Izzy raised her hands and grunted to be released from her highchair, and he unbuckled the safety belt and lifted her into his arms. "And speaking of work, we'd better get back to our pirate ship."

Max raced ahead of them into the family room.

"Thank you," Lorna said quietly, nudging her

shoulder into his. "I already made you something to say thank you for last night. It was kind of a surprise, but now I'm going to have to think of another way to thank you for helping me at the shop."

He narrowed his eyes, noticing how close she was still standing to him. "First of all, I love surprises. But you've got me more intrigued by this offer of *another way* to thank me. Not that you *have* to thank me, but what did you have in mind?"

And by any chance did it involve her wrapping those luscious legs around his waist?

Oh no. Settle down there, stallion.

Being friends didn't usually involve the kind of things he was imagining. Although she *had* been kind of flirty tonight, so maybe she might consider being friends...*with benefits.*

The teasing grin on her lips told him she knew exactly what he was thinking. "How about we just focus on the surprise?" She went into the kitchen and brought back a plastic tub with a blue lid. "I made these for you this morning."

Mack shifted the baby on his hip so he could open the lid, and the delicious scents of peanut butter and chocolate wafted up to him. "You made me cookies?"

"Yeah, I saw that Reese's wrapper in your truck, so I figured you must like peanut butter and chocolate, so these are basically chocolate chip cookies with peanut butter chips mixed in as well."

"Wow. I don't know what to say. No one's ever made cookies just for me before." He gingerly lifted one out and stared at it. "Damn, I'm trying not to get choked up over a simple baked good, but this means a lot."

"I'm glad," she whispered, smiling up at him. And danged if her eyes weren't a little teary.

He stuffed the cookie in his mouth, partly because it smelled so good, and partly to keep him from telling her he'd just fallen in love with her. He groaned at the mouthwatering flavors of vanilla, peanut butter, and chocolate. The cookie was just the right mix of chewy and crunchy, and he reached for a second one. "These are amazing."

"Yeah?" She smiled up at him, but still a question hung in her eyes. "You really like them?"

"Hell yes, I do." He grinned around another bite. "They kind of remind me of you. A little salty, a little sweet, kind of gooey on the inside, and just looking at them, I know they're gonna taste delicious."

She laughed. "You have quite the mouth on you." Her gaze dropped to his lips and a rush of heat surged through him.

He leaned close to her neck, close enough for the scent of her to surround him and make his head a little dizzy. "Just say the word, and it could be on you."

Her eyes widened, and pink flared her cheeks as a naughty grin teased the corners of her lips.

She's considering it. Score one for the cowboy.

She looked up at him from below her long eyelashes, a coy smile on her lips. "You do tempt me, Mack Lassiter," she whispered.

His gaze dropped to her lips.

Speaking of tempting.

She swallowed then pulled her bottom lip under her front teeth, and he almost groaned as hard as he had with the bite of cookie. He knew she would taste just as good.

It was taking everything in him not to cover her mouth with his. Although, the baby on his hip and the container of cookies were impeding him from slipping an arm around her waist and pulling her to him, he was still thinking about how good she felt against him.

"Come on, you guys," Max called from the family room. "This pirate ship isn't going to build itself."

Mack breathed out a laugh, the moment broken, but he was pretty sure he'd still be thinking about her lips and the way her teeth bit into her bottom one when he was trying to fall asleep that night.

Lorna tilted her head. "We'd better get in there."

"Yup," he said, then lowered his voice as he leaned closer. "But just so you know, the booty on that pirate ship isn't the only super sexy one I'm thinking about."

She laughed out loud, giving her hips a little extra wiggle as she turned and walked toward the family room.

He laughed with her then tried to turn his focus to the remaining Lego's left on the table. "It seemed like we were making such good process, so why does it feel like there are more pieces here than when we went in for supper?"

"Because there is over a thousand pieces to this thing," Lorna said. "But I appreciate that you got Max something that would challenge him, instead of assuming he needed something smaller."

"And if we don't finish," Max said, his focus still on

the tiny cannon he was piecing together. "You'll just have to come back over again tomorrow."

Mack raised an eyebrow at Lorna.

She shrugged. "It's up to you. I'm fixing tacos."

He grinned, deciding that he needed to slow down the assembling process to insure they didn't finish that night. "Another one of my favorite meals."

Izzy was sitting in his lap again, and she squinched her face together for a moment then gurgled out a happy grin as the source of that smile wafted through the air.

"Oh yuck," Max said, waving his hand in front of his face. "Izzy pooped."

"Everybody poops, bud," Mack responded, unfazed by the baby's fragrant odor. "And cowboys see a lot of it. Cow poop, pig poop, chicken poop. Just this morning, I was cleaning out piles of horse poop that were bigger than your head."

Max giggled.

"Did you know that because elephants only digest about forty-five percent of their food, and their poop is mostly made up of fiber, that an Elephant Conservation Center in Thailand created a method for making elephant dung into paper," Mack told him. "They clean the fibers first then process them and turn them into handmade notebooks. One elephant can poop enough to make over a hundred pages of paper a day."

"I don't know if I'd want to write on paper made from poop." Max scrunched up his forehead as if considering the idea. "It sounds kind of gross."

"I think it sounds pretty cool that they figured out

a way to make something useful from waste," Mack said. "But if you really want to hear something gross, they also make a really expensive coffee from beans that are collected from the poop of an animal in Asai called a palm civet."

"Coffee from poop?" Max did the bones-to-jelly move as he slid his body off the sofa and onto the floor. Then he looked up at his mom. "Is that true? Do you have poop coffee at your shop."

Lorna laughed. "Yes, it's true. But no, I do not serve that kind of coffee. For one thing, it's ridiculously expensive, and I've heard it's more of a gimmicky thing, and doesn't even taste that great. And I've also heard that they aren't very kind to the animals that make it." She glanced over at Mack. "I'm kind of impressed with your vast knowledge of poo trivia."

"That's how I usually win over the ladies," he said, then couldn't hold a straight face and busted out a laugh. "Really, I'm just good at remembering weird facts. I could tell you a ton of other things about scat. You just never know when a piece of that kind of odd trivia might come in handy."

Lorna laughed with him. "Do you get into a lot of conversations where you need to pull out this trove of poop-related trivia?"

He offered her a mischievous grin. "I'm in one right now." He lifted Izzy up. "You want me to change her?"

Lorna shook her head as she stood and took the baby from him. "No, I've got it. But the fact that you offered is noted."

The sound of the front door opening had Lorna

turning her head then the very air in the room changed as a man's voice called out, "Honey I'm home...."

Chapter Ten

LORNA'S MOUTH WENT dry and every muscle in her body tightened. The spaghetti in her stomach churned and roiled and threatened to come back up.

She hadn't seen him in a year and a half, but she knew that voice—that mocking tone laced with underlying menace.

Her body shrunk into itself—the way it had for the full five years of their marriage—as if only she could make herself smaller, which was laughable for a curvy woman who stood over five feet eight inches tall, then maybe he wouldn't notice her. Or he might leave her alone.

But it had never worked.

And it was *not* working now.

She breathed out his name. "Lyle." Forcing back the wave of panic that threatened to consume her, she flashed a hard stare at Mack then at her son then back to the cowboy. "Stay here," she commanded, then hurried down the hallway, her primary goal to keep her ex away from the family room and Max.

She tried to keep the fear—the emotion that like

a vampire to a drop of blood—he most liked to feed on, tamped down as the man she'd given six years of her life to walked into the kitchen at the same time she did.

He looked a little different—his dark hair was cut into a trendier style, and he may have lost a few pounds. She imagined those were both due to him trying to keep up with a younger girlfriend. Same with his clothes, tan golf shorts and a red polo shirt that was still a little too tight around his bulging middle. Maybe he'd changed, but she'd never known him to play a round of golf. Although, his outfit also made her think of someone who might help her find the laundry detergent at Target.

He was a few years older and had played defensive end for their high school football team. A few inches shy of six feet, he'd once had the body, and the strength of an athlete, but he'd let his workouts go after they'd gotten married and packed on an extra fifty pounds. Which, of course, he'd blamed on her for feeding him too much. And despite losing his athleticism, he still had plenty of strength, as her blackened eyes and split lips had proved.

She swallowed and tried to force some pleasantness into her tone. He'd always hated sarcasm or when she'd questioned some decision he'd made. "Hey Lyle. What are you doing here?"

He cocked an eyebrow and brandished that expression he used to make right before he asked her if she was stupid. "I just told you. I'm home."

The word sent a chill racing down her spine.

"This is not your home," she wanted to scream.

But she knew—as sure as she knew how to back

slowly away from a rattlesnake coiled in the middle of a hiking path—to do the same with that comment. The wrong word or any sudden movement could cause the snake—and Lyle—to strike.

"Where's Misty?" she asked, trying to keep her tone light as she peered behind him for the petite younger blond woman he'd left his family for. He was such a cliché, running off with the administrative assistant at the insurance company they'd both worked at.

Wrong question.

His brow furrowed as a dark expression crossed his face. "You don't need to worry about Misty. She's taken care of. But something smells real good in here, so maybe you *could* worry about fixing me up a plate."

Taken care of?

What the hell did that mean? That she'd already eaten? Or that he had left her, too? Or did *taken care of* mean his violent temper had finally killed someone?

"Oh, sorry, there's none left." She knew that Mack had stuck a container of leftover spaghetti in the refrigerator and that she was taking a risk by not offering Lyle some. It would really piss him off if he checked the fridge and found the container.

But her main objective was just to get him out of the house, so she wasn't about to offer him a plate of supper if she could help it.

His gaze roamed around the room. She fought another shudder as it felt like he was cataloging and appraising the value of everything she owned.

"Pretty fancy digs. It would have been nice if your mom would've offered us this place back when we were barely making rent in that shitty apartment we used to live in."

Except my mom couldn't stand you.

"I notice that you failed to mention owning this house in the divorce settlement." He said the words lightly, but she could hear the sneer and contempt in his tone.

"I *don't* own this house. It's still my mom's. She's just letting us live here."

He paused in his appraisal and cocked his head at her. "Rent free, I suppose."

Izzy had been holding still in Lorna's arms as if she could sense the distress of her mother. Her eyes were wide as she watched this strange man posture around their living room then she buried her face in Lorna's shoulder.

Lyle finally looked at the child in her arms. "I guess it's about time I met my daughter. She's pretty cute. Must have got that from my side of the family." He reached his arms out for the baby. "Come here, Elizabeth. Come to Daddy."

Lorna gritted her teeth so hard she feared one of her molars might crack. "Her name is *Isabel.*"

The baby shrank against her—like mother, like daughter—and whimpered as Lyle plucked her from Lorna's arms.

"That's what I said. Isabel." He started to put her on his hip then wrinkled his nose and made a gagging sound as he shoved her back at Lorna. "Good Lord, she reeks. Does she always smell like that?"

She caught herself right before rolling her eyes—she'd learned the hard way how Lyle felt about that action. "No."

He fanned his hand in front of his face. "Damn,

I forgot how bad a shitty diaper smells. Don't you change her?"

"Of course I do. I was just getting ready to when you let yourself into my house."

"Don't you mean *our* house?"

Bile rose in her throat.

He gestured back toward the living room. "I just need to grab my stuff from the car. I'm good taking the couch tonight though. For now."

She swallowed hard, trying to think of something, *anything*, to say that wouldn't set him off.

But there was no way in hell she was letting him back into her house.

Or her life.

She tried to keep her tone calm. "No. I mean, I don't think that's gonna work."

His eyes narrowed, and his tone hardened as he took a menacing step toward her. "No? What's the problem?"

"I think the lady said no," a low voice stated from behind her.

Shit.

She appreciated Mack standing up for her, but she didn't want to give Lyle a reason to get angry. She just wanted him out of her house. Although it didn't seem like he was planning on going anywhere.

Lyle's gaze flashed toward the tall cowboy who came to stand next to her. "Who the hell are you?"

"Mack Lassiter." He extended his hand. Lorna waited—*and wished*—for Mack to crush Lyle's in a hard vise grip.

But her ex just looked at Mack's offered hand with

disdain, as if it were holding out a dog turd in his palm. "And what are you doing in my wife's house?"

"*Ex*-wife," she and Mack said at the same time.

Mack took Lorna's hand, squeezing it in silent support, and she held onto him as if he were a life preserver and she'd just been thrown into a shark-infested sea. Except there was only one shark, and she wasn't sure that even a six-foot something life preserver could save her from it.

"He's mommy's friend," Max said, his small chin raised as he stepped in front of Mack.

Lyle's gaze turned sharp, glancing from the boy to the man behind him then dropping to their joined hands between them. His lips curled into a sneer. "I didn't realize Mommy had *a friend*."

"I wouldn't think she'd need to inform you about *anything* she had," Mack told him. "The two of you are divorced, so she can have any kind of friend she wants."

Lyle's sneer fixed on Lorna. "I think you need to tell your boyfriend to stand down."

"I don't need to tell my boyfriend anything," she said, pushing her shoulders back as she drew strength from the squeeze of Mack's hand. "He can do what he wants. But he *is* the reason you can't stay here."

Lyle's gaze went back and forth between them as if assessing the situation, then he held his hands up in surrender. "Hey, no problem. I'll find someplace else to stay tonight. But we've got things we need to talk about, so I'll be back tomorrow."

"Make sure you call first," Mack told him.

She stood still, clinging to Mack's hand, as Lyle backed out of the room. Then she let out a breath she hadn't realized she was holding when the sound of the door slamming echoed through the house.

"You guys okay?" Mack asked, reaching for her son's hand and drawing him closer to them, the concern for *all* of them etched on his face.

That might have been the moment she fell in love with him.

She nodded, but her voice seemed to have deserted her.

He pulled her in, holding her and Izzy against his shoulder while Max wrapped his arms around their legs, hugging them both at the same time. She let go of Mack's hand to grip her son's shoulder.

"I'm sorry," she whispered into the soft flannel of his shirt.

"What the hell for? You didn't do anything."

"For insinuating you were my boyfriend. It just sort of came out."

He shrugged. "It's fine. I'll be whatever you need me to be if it helps get rid of that jerk. Did you know he was in town?"

She shook her head. "I had no idea."

"The nerve of that guy. Walking in here and acting like he was going to stay."

She could feel the tautness of Mack's shoulders, the anger humming through his body. She recognized the emotion—the fury that Lyle incited.

"He didn't even say hello to Max," she said softly, choking back a sob. "Or try to hug him. He hasn't seen his son in a year and a half, and he barely acknowledged his presence."

Don't you dare let him make you cry.

She swallowed back the tears, but her body betrayed

her as her hands trembled, and she squeezed them into tight fists.

"It's okay, darlin'. I got you. All three of you. And you don't have to worry. He's gone now."

Yeah, he was gone *now*, but like a bad penny, she had this terrible imminent feeling he would show up again.

Chapter Eleven

Mack held back a yawn the next afternoon as he wiped down the front counter of the coffee shop. The morning had been busy, and he'd kept at it all day, but thanks to the fact that he'd stayed in town until close to midnight so he could drive by Lorna's house several times just in case her jerk of an ex-husband decided to make another appearance, and then gotten up extra early to get his chores done so he could be at the coffeeshop by seven, meant he hadn't gotten much sleep.

It had been a fun day with Lorna though.

She'd gone through the basic menu with him when he arrived that morning and showed him how to run the register and mark the hot or cold cups with the customers' names and the codes for their orders. She'd even talked him into wearing one of the shop's pink polo shirts that had the Mountain Brew logo across the breast pocket.

Although he had enjoyed teasing her by pulling his T-shirt off in front of her and offering her a couple of bicep flexes as he took his time donning the new shirt.

He loved the sneaky little grin that played at the corners of her lips as she'd feigned disinterest, but he still caught her looking.

Growing up, he'd been a skinny kid who'd probably bordered on malnourished, thanks to his mom's frequent absences, an empty pantry, and a growth spurt in seventh grade, but he'd gotten his first job on a ranch when he was seventeen and the abundance of healthy meals and the tasks and responsibilities of a cowboy had filled his body out and created strong muscles that he'd earned with every toss of a hay bale or swing of a hammer.

He saw himself as kind of average looking, and he knew the strength of his body, which gave him the ability to help out on the ranch and with the chores, but he still liked that a cheap flex made Lorna smile and caused her to get a bit flustered. Like the way she dropped the measuring cup when she tried to show him how to use the bean grinder.

Most of the coffee drinks started with at least one shot of espresso, so after he'd changed, she taught him how to use the espresso machine and the differences between lattes, cappuccinos, and iced coffee drinks.

He had eventually worked up to frothing milk and plating croissants and baked goods, but he was also happy to bus and wipe tables and restock napkins and stir sticks. It didn't matter what he was doing, it just made him happy to be helping her.

And it was fun watching her work.

Besides how cute she looked in her navy apron, pink shirt, white sneakers, and snug ankle length jeans that hugged her generous hips, she had a great rapport with customers. He couldn't get enough of hearing her laugh, and there was a practiced flow to her movements as she mixed and poured and created frothy drinks that she presented with care and love.

She knew almost everyone who came in and was adept at remembering the way they liked their coffee and their names, as well as those of their family members. And he loved how she snuck dog biscuits from the glass jar under the counter to the four-legged friends who accompanied some of them.

The whole culture of a coffee shop had changed over the last decade, and it was now somewhere to be, to hang out, to meet friends, to hold meetings, to go on dates. It was more about community, and there was something unique and special about handing someone a drink specifically made for them.

"I have to admit, I haven't spent a lot of time in a coffee shop before today," he told Lorna during one of their breaks. "But I like your place. It has a good feel about it."

She grinned over at him. "Thank you. I try really hard to create that neighborhood 'coffee with a friend' vibe. And it means a lot to have a non-coffee shop guy get that."

"I do. You've created a space where people are comfortable working or just hanging out, and it's been fun people-watching and eavesdropping on conversations all day. There was that one couple, with the girl in the green dress, who I couldn't figure out if they were on a first date or a job interview."

She laughed. "I was wondering about them, too."

"It's been fun working with you, as well." Fun, and a little frustrating.

Working in such tight quarters and smelling her

hair and her perfume as she rushed past him, had him constantly trying to find ways to be close to her. The space behind the counter wasn't very wide, so it seemed like they were constantly bumping into each other or brushing against the other one.

It was amazing.

And maddening.

He nudged her with his hip. "You're pretty impressive."

"Thanks. So are you. I'm surprised at how quickly you picked things up today. You've been a huge help. Especially this morning when Max was still here. You're really good with him. And it helped that I didn't have to close the shop to run him the few blocks to school."

"He's a good kid. And funny. He makes me laugh. And finding odd little jobs for him to do was much easier than trying to stall that customer who came in while you were gone. Because I had *zero* idea of how to make the grande half-caf skim-milk five-tears-of-a-dragon drink he ordered."

Lorna laughed. "Yeah, that five-tears-of-a-dragon latte is one of our more complicated ones."

"I don't know how you keep them all straight. Or how your employees do. Plus, all the other things you do here."

"Mainly because I have an OCD rocket scientist for a sister who filled in here when I had Izzy, and she created plans and lists and a book of procedures for everything from opening to closing to recipes for all the drink options." She pulled a laminated deck of colorful cards on a binder ring from under the counter. "I was going to wait to show you this until tomorrow, but these cards explain how to make all the drinks we offer, complete with illustrations and detailed instructions."

"What?" He flipped through the cards. "These are amazing."

"I know. Leni made them. They've helped my employees so much."

"I kind of want to take these home and study them, so I'll be a bigger help tomorrow."

She took the cards from him and stuck them back under the counter. "No homework. You don't have to learn everything all at once. And you've already helped so much."

He pressed his lips together to keep from arguing and shoved his hands in his pockets so he wouldn't be tempted to pull the cards back out and study them. He had pitched in as a warm body today, but if he knew the recipes, then he could be an even bigger help the next day.

He liked helping people, especially gorgeous curvy single mom's whose scent drove him to distraction.

But Mack had also found, in his life, that people seemed to like having him around more when he was helping them. No one wanted a stray kid around who just got in the way, but most everyone appreciated him if he was pitching in or making their life easier.

It was almost two, and Lorna had told him she liked to close then so she had time to clean up before getting Max from school at two-thirty.

Most of the customers had left for the day, and Mack was collecting trash and wiping down the tables in the lobby. One woman was reading a book as she finished a slice of coffee cake, and there was one guy who'd had his laptop open and his golden retriever sleeping on his feet under the table while he'd been working for the last three hours. He'd ordered food and two coffees though and must have been a regular the way he joked around with Lorna and ordered his 'usual'.

The table in the corner held an older woman, who'd introduced herself to Mack earlier as Judy Fitzgerald, and her eight-year-old grandson, Dylan. They ordered hot chocolates with extra whipped cream and split a large slice of vanilla cake with white frosting and had been chatting and laughing while playing cards for the last hour.

Mack paused to check in on them as he passed their table. "You all doin' okay? Can I get you anything else?"

"I think we're good," Judy told him. She looked to be in her mid-sixties, with a curly bob of blond and gray hair, but seemed young at heart in a pair of jeans, sneakers, and a pink sweatshirt that read '*In my Grandma Era*' on the front. "Except I've just lost six straight games to this guy. It's a good thing we're only wagering gummy worms."

The boy shrugged at Mack. He had a slight build, light blond hair, and wore small wire-rimmed glasses and a Spiderman T-shirt. "I can't help it if I'm good at Blackjack."

He laughed, assuming earlier that they'd been playing some kind of kid's card game instead of the Las Vegas staple.

"I'm glad to have finally met you today," Judy said. "I've known Duke for years, and he speaks highly of you. I know he's excited you've moved out to the ranch with him."

"Thank you, ma'am. I'm excited too. I really love it out there."

Dylan was staring up at him. "Are you a real cowboy?"

"Yup. Got my own horse and everything."

"I think I might want to be a cowboy when I grow up," the boy told him. "Either that, or an astronaut."

"Well, either one of those would be a fine profession. Although I believe one takes a considerable amount more training than the other and probably pays a lot more. But if you're interested in rockets, you should talk to Lorna's sister, Leni. She builds them for a living."

"Rockets are cool," Dylan agreed. "But so are horses."

"Dylan's been wanting to take horseback riding lessons," Judy explained. "But we haven't found a place yet that offers them."

"If you want to ride a horse, you're welcome to come out to the ranch anytime and ride one of ours," Mack said. "We've got an older mare who's a real sweet pony and would be perfect for a kid to learn on."

Dylan's eyes lit up. "Can we, Grandma?"

Judy frowned. "I'm not sure. How much would you charge for lessons?"

Mack waved away her comment. "I wouldn't charge anything. Heck, I can remember being a kid and wanting to learn to ride a horse. It would be fun. Come out anytime."

"Thank you," Judy said. "That's a kind offer."

"I mean it." He started to move to wipe down the next table, then turned back to them. "You know what? I hate those open-ended offers where the other person is never quite sure how to really take someone up on them. So, let's just set a time now. How about some afternoon this week? The shop is closed on Wednesday, so I should be at the ranch most of the day."

Dylan bounced up and down in his seat. "Can we? Please? Please?"

Judy frowned. "I work on Wednesday. I *could* try to take a long lunch hour, but you've got school."

"It's the second to last day, and we've got a sub this week," Dylan said. "And she already said we're going to be watching a movie every day after lunch, so I wouldn't miss anything if you took me out early for just one afternoon."

"We can do it sometime next week," Mack offered. "I'll be around."

Judy studied her grandson then let out an exaggerated sigh. "Far be it from me, and a substitute teacher who thinks watching movies is teaching, to stand in the way of a dream to be a cowboy. I'll take a late lunch and excuse you from school for the last hour and a half. Just this once."

"Yay!" Dylan popped out of his seat to give his grandmother a hug. "Thank you, Grandma."

She looked at Mack and shrugged. "I'm a sucker for a grandson hug. Around one-thirty then?" She pulled a business card from her purse and passed it to Mack. "My cell phone is on there. You can call or text me if it's not going to work out."

"That sounds great," Mack told her. "I can't imagine

it wouldn't, but I can give you my number as well." He took the pen and notepad that she and Dylan had been keeping score on and jotted down his cell number. "See you Wednesday."

"I caught the tail end of that conversation," Lorna said when he walked back to the front counter where she was restocking cups. "That was a pretty nice thing you offered."

He shrugged off her compliment, even though it secretly pleased him. "They seem nice. And I think it's cool the kid spends time with his grandmother."

Lorna lowered her voice to a whisper. "They spend *all* their time together. Dylan's mom has a lot of problems, and Judy's had custody of him since he was born."

"That's impressive."

"She's a neat lady. She's been with the Clerk and Recorders office at the courthouse for close to thirty years, she volunteers at the library, and she's coached Dylan's soccer team for the last two seasons."

"Wow. Now I'm even more impressed. I always wanted a grandma, but I missed out on ever knowing any of my grandparents. Until Duke."

"I think he's planning to make that up to you."

The bell above the door jangled, and the smile fell from Lorna's face as she looked toward the front of the store.

"Shit," she whispered. "What is he doing here?"

Mack turned to see Lyle strolling toward them, a calculating grin on his face as he eyed the interior of the shop. "Damn. This is a pretty nice place you've got here, Lorna," he said, slapping a hand on the counter.

Mack hated the way Lorna flinched at the sound of

the slap, and he wondered if Lyle had used that same motion on her. The thought of him laying a hand on Lorna, or God forbid, Max, had the blood boiling under Mack's skin.

He casually dropped his arm around Lorna's shoulder, both to offer her support and to show Lyle his presence wasn't affecting him. "Sorry, pal. We just cleaned the espresso machine, and we're closing up for the day. But they serve coffee and pie at the diner down the street."

"I'm not as interested in a cup of coffee as I am in this coffee *shop*. This building's gotta be worth quite a chunk of change." He narrowed his eyes at Lorna. "You win the lottery after you divorced me?" His eyes cut to Mack. "Or did you buy this place for her?"

"She did every bit of this on her own," he said. "And this place belongs solely to her."

"We'll see about that," Lyle said, and Mack wanted to smack the derisive smirk off his face. He turned away, but called over his shoulder, "We're gonna have that talk soon, Lorna. Sometime when your boyfriend isn't around."

Like hell you are.

Chapter Twelve

Mack's arm tightened around Lorna. The air in the coffee shop seemed to cool ten degrees as the door closed behind Lyle, and her shoulders released a hard shudder.

The four remaining patrons were all staring at Lorna, and he turned his body to block their view as he pulled her to him. "You okay?"

Her eyes were wide as she stared up at him. "He's gonna try to take my shop."

Mack was thinking the same thing.

Greedy bastard.

"He's an asshole."

"Agreed." She pulled away, sucking in a long breath then pushing back her shoulders. She pulled a set of keys from her pocket and handed it to him. "Will you lock up after everyone leaves? I'm going to take the trash out and clear my head for a minute."

"Yeah, you got it. Take all the time you need."

The woman with the book offered a small wave as dumped her empty cup and plate and slipped out the door, but Judy, Dylan, and the young guy with the golden retriever, who Lorna had told him was named Nick, all came up to the counter after Lorna left.

"Is she all right?" Judy asked, worry etched on her face.

"That guy was a douche," Nick said. "Even my dog thought so, and she likes everyone."

"She will be," Mack told them, appreciating their concern.

"I didn't realize you two were dating," Judy said, reaching out to pat his hand. "But I'm glad she has you."

Nick nodded. "Me too. Take care of her, dude. She's a great person."

"I will," he told them, and meant it with every fiber of his being.

He locked up after them and finished wiping down the tables, then started to worry that Lorna hadn't come back. Pushing through the back door, he was surprised to see a small patio area in the alleyway behind the shop. A seating area with a wrought-iron table, an umbrella, and two matching chairs was to the left as he walked out, and a stack of wooden pallets were lined up behind the door.

But instead of sitting in one of the chairs, Lorna was crouched on the ground by the pallets holding a dog biscuit out to a small scruffy brown and black dog. The dog gingerly took the biscuit then inched back into what Mack now saw was a small crate with a gray blanket tucked into it and a water dish in front of it.

"I didn't know you had a dog," Mack said, crouching down next to her.

"I don't," she said. "She's just a stray. I found her

behind the shop a few weeks ago, but she wouldn't let me get close enough to pet her or take her to the shelter. I've been setting out food and water and trying to get her to trust me, but so far, no luck."

"She's a cute little bugger," Mack said, tilting his head and holding his hand out toward the dog. But the animal only pulled further back into the crate. "What's her name?"

"I told you, she's not mine."

"You put a blanket in a crate and you're feeding her on a regular basis. In dog terms, she's yours."

She let out a huff. "I've been calling her Mocha. Because I found her behind the shop, I thought she needed a coffee-inspired name, and her coloring makes me think of creamed coffee and chocolate."

"I like it." He stood and gestured to the door. "I locked up and finished wiping down the tables. Anything else I can do to help?"

She shook her head as she stood too. Then she let out a heavy sigh and slumped down into one of the chairs. "I don't know how, but he's gonna get this place from me. I can feel it in my gut."

He pulled the other chair around and sat down so he was facing her, their knees almost touching. "He might try, but he has no legal right to it. From what I remember you telling me, your grandmother left you this place after Lyle was gone. Was it included in the divorce settlement?"

She shook her head. "No. My grandma was smart. Smarter than me. She saw through Lyle's bullshit, and she made sure that the building would only come to me. And all the legal transfer of ownership happened after the divorce had been finalized."

"Damn. I'm amazed you got this place up and running while you were pregnant."

"Me too. But I wanted it so bad. And I've never been afraid of hard work." A sad smile played around the edges of her lips. "My grandma used to want to have tea parties with me, and I'd always turn it around, so I was the shop owner, and she had to come and order and buy the tea from me before we could sit down and drink it. It was all with pretend money, but I've just always loved the idea of running a little shop that sold coffee and tea and croissants and tiny cakes."

"And now you're doing it."

Her eyes got a far away look in them. "I built this place all by myself. And I've run it successfully for over a year now. It's something that's all mine. That *he* isn't a part of and hasn't tainted with insults about the shop or about how stupid I am or how I have no idea how to run a business. Sure, I've made some dumb mistakes, like not knowing how much milk to order when we first opened and getting the wrong kind of syrup, but I figured out how to fix them on my own and learn from them."

"You don't have to convince me. I'm in awe of what you've done here. You've built something that's more than just a coffee shop, it's a community."

Her gaze swung back to him, and she stared at him for a moment, studying his face as if gauging the sincerity of his words, then she pushed out of her chair and landed in his lap, wrapping her hands around his head and pulling his face toward her as she pressed a hard kiss to his lips.

Surprise and shock gave way to need and passion as his arms wrapped around her back, pulling her closer as he tilted his head and deepened the kiss. She moaned against his mouth, a small kitten whimper that had him instantly rock hard, and one of his hands slid down to cup her perfectly round ass.

She shifted in his lap, pressing her center against the length of him, and his palm tightened the hold he had on her butt as his tongue slipped between her lips. She tasted like coffee and chocolate—and desire—and he couldn't get enough of her.

One of her hands clutched his back while the other dug through his hair, gripping handfuls of it as she kissed him harder, deeper, with more intensity.

Everything else fell away. He was completely lost in her.

He wanted more, *needed* more. He had to touch her, feel her skin.

His hand slid under her shirt, skimming over her waist. He caught her quick inhale of breath as his fingers stretched across her lower back and pulled her closer still.

The beep-beep of a horn from a car driving by in the alley had them pulling apart and Lorna pushed off his lap as if it had suddenly caught fire. Which, there was a strong chance that it had.

She offered the car a little embarrassed wave then smoothed down her apron as she turned to go back into the coffee shop. "I've got to pick Max up from school."

Ooh-kay.

Apparently, they were going to act like that hadn't just happened. Like she didn't just rock his frickin' world by landing in his lap and kissing him senseless.

Adjusting himself as he stood, he tried to catch his

breath as he followed her into the shop. "You want me to walk down to the school with you?"

She wasn't wasting any time. She'd already taken off her apron and gotten her purse from the back office, and she busied herself with putting the last few things away on the counter then heading for the front door, all while seemingly trying to avoid his eye. "No, I'm good. Thank you though. I've taken up so much of your day already."

He passed her the keys for the door that she'd given him earlier. "It's been fun. I like hanging out with you."

And kissing you.

He *really* liked that. But he truly enjoyed just being in her company. She made him laugh, and he felt at ease around her.

She unlocked the door, waited for them both to exit then locked it again, all still without looking at him. After dropping the keys in her purse, she finally raised her eyes to meet his, although he could swear she hesitated just for a second on his lips before she met his gaze. "Do you still want to come over for tacos tonight? I know Max is bugging you to help with the pirate ship, but I don't want you to feel obligated."

He stepped closer to her, sensing that like he would treat a skittish colt, he needed to move slowly, as he gently raised his hand to her shoulder. "Yes, I would love to still come over for tacos. And Max is not bugging me. Not at all. I'm looking forward to it." He slid his hand closer so that his palm cupped her neck as he eased her chin up with his thumb and searched her eyes for answers to what was upsetting her. "You okay?"

"Yes. No." She reached up to clutch the hand holding her neck. "I'm not sure. I told you I'm a hot mess, and I don't want to give you mixed signals, I just…you're being so nice to me…and I'm used to doing everything on my own…and you've really stepped up…and you were saying all the right things…and my god, you're so damn hot…and oh, hell, I don't know…"

"Hey, it's all right," he said softly, trying not to get hung up on the part where she thought he was *so damn hot*. "We're okay. I mean, that was one *hell* of a kiss, and I think I'm still recovering from you knocking me a little senseless, but I'm still here. For as long as you want me to be. And for whatever you need."

"Thank you," she whispered, as she leaned her cheek onto his hand and closed her eyes for just a moment before pulling away from him and fussing with the strap of her purse. "I'll see you later. For tacos. Around five?"

"I'll be there."

Wild horses couldn't keep him away.

Chapter Thirteen

THE TACOS HAD been delicious, but all Mack could think of was their earlier kiss as he helped Lorna clear the table and fill the dishwasher. He almost dropped a plate when she bent over to pick up one of the three spoons Izzy had dropped on the floor.

She'd changed into black leggings, a pink cami, and a loose sweatshirt that kept sliding off one shoulder—which drove him nuts every time it did.

He loved her body—the lushness of it, the curves he imagined exploring, and all he wanted was to pull her against him and slide his lips over the creamy skin of her bare shoulder.

They'd been a little careful around each other tonight. He was still very aware of when they were in each other's space and when her hip or shoulder brushed his, but he was doing his best to be thoughtful and easy and not bulldoze her with all the feelings and desire trying to bust out of him.

"I wanted to give Izzy a bath tonight. The warm water helps her sleep, and the steam is good for her ears," Lorna told him when they'd finished the kitchen. "Would you be willing to hang out with Max a bit longer so I can get her bathed and put to bed?"

"Heck, yeah." He nodded toward the family room. "We've still got more work to do on the pirate ship."

Max shook his head. "I don't want to work on it without Mommy. It's a family project."

The sentiment hit Mack hard. The kid had no idea what it meant to him to be included in any kind of mention of family. "What do you want to do then?"

"Do you know how to play checkers?" Max asked.

"Course."

Lorena chuckled. "Probably not the way Max does." She picked Izzy up and balanced her on one jutted hip. "Good luck."

Mack figured out what she meant ten minutes later when Max had set up the board and they had started to play.

"King me," the boy said, after going back to the same spot where he'd already gotten a second black checker stacked on his first one.

"I already did," Mack told him.

"I know, but I landed here again," the boy explained as if it made perfect sense.

"Are you just making up your own rules?"

Max shrugged and offered him an impish grin. "It's our game. That means we can make up the rules and play it however we want."

"You can't argue his point," Lorna said, as she passed through the room with a wiggling baby wrapped in a towel in one arm and a stack of clean pajamas she'd just grabbed from the dryer in the other.

Mack stared across the board at his pint-sized opponent.

When in Rome...

He placed another black piece on top of the boy's already double-stacked checkers. Then he picked up his red piece, hopped over two of Max's black ones, then lifted the checker up and spun it around the board twice before landing in one of the farthest spaces. "All right, king me too."

Max cocked a small eyebrow as he stared down at the board, then back up at Mack.

"I call that the helicopter move," he said in a serious tone, and waited for the boy to challenge him.

Max studied the board then his face creased with a wide grin. "I *like* it," he said and slammed a red checker on top of the one Mack had landed. He picked up the rest of the red ones he'd won and crowned three more of Mack's checkers that were in various spots on the board. "I win."

"How do you figure?"

The boy held up his empty hands. "I'm out of checkers."

Mack laughed, completely bewildered and besotted with this adorable kid.

"Wanna play again?" Max asked.

"No."

The boy's face fell.

"But I have a new game. Have you ever played *Chuckers*?"

His face brightened. "No. How do you play?"

"First, you have to go get the biggest bowl you can find," Mack instructed.

The boy raced into the kitchen and came back a minute later with a large pink Tupperware bowl.

He'd had the same one growing up, except it was a faded gummy yellow, and served as the combination popcorn, pasta salad, and puke bowl. "Perfect. Now go stand over there," Mack told him, pointing to the other side of the room then scooping a handful of checkers off the board. "And I'm going to start chucking these checkers and you try to catch them in the bowl."

By the time Lorna came downstairs ten minutes later, the bowl had been forgotten, and the carpet was littered with black and red checkers as the game had lapsed into just the two of them hurling the pieces at each other in a version of 'Dodge Checkers'.

She raised an eyebrow at Mack as her son dove for cover from another checker onslaught. "Is this your idea of calming him down to go to sleep?"

He ducked as a red piece sailed past his ear. "Checkers with this kid didn't feel like a calm activity in the first place. Have you ever played with him?"

She barked out a laugh. "Oh yes, many times."

"This isn't checkers," Max called from his spot behind the chair. "It's *Chuckers*. Mack taught me."

She offered a questioning glance at Mack. "What's Chuckers?"

"Instead of playing *with* the checkers on the board, you chuck 'em *at* each other," Max yelled then fell into a fit of giggles as he crawled out from behind the sofa and flung a black game piece in Mack's direction.

Lorna ducked. "Super idea."

"It started out that we were just trying to chuck

them into a bowl," Mack explained, sticking his hand out to catch a checker in midair before it hit Lorna.

The doorbell rang before Mack had a chance to justify his newly invented game, and he was surprised to see Dodge and Maisie standing on the doorstep.

"Sorry to stop by unannounced," Maisie said. "But we were coming home from dinner and saw Mack's truck parked outside and decided we should stop and have a chat."

"Hey brother," Dodge said, stepping inside and nodding to Mack.

"It's no trouble," Lorna said. Over the last year, she and Leni had become quite good friends with Maisie and Ford's girlfriend, Elizabeth, and they often hung out at Lorna's house, drinking wine and chatting after the kids had gone to bed. "You know you're both welcome here anytime."

Dodge's huge black dog, Moose, stood obediently on the doorstep, waiting for an invitation to come inside. Lorna opened the door wider and beckoned the dog into the living room, where Moose made a beeline for Max, who fell on the floor, giggling as the dog covered him in slobbery puppy kisses.

"Can I take Moose upstairs to my room?" Max asked his mother.

"Sure, honey," Lorna said. "But only if you promise to put your pj's on and then read him some books. And *not* be rowdy. Your sister is asleep."

"I promise," the boy said, holding one finger to his lips to shush the giant dog as it followed him up the stairs.

"So, what's up?" Mack asked when they were gone,

knowing his brother well enough by now to see that something was going on.

"Not sure if you were aware, but you two seem to be the talk of the town today," Dodge told them.

"Us?" Lorna asked. "Why?"

Dodge aimed a good-natured grin in Mack's direction. "Oh, for so many reasons. Starting with the fact that somebody caught you two making out in the alley behind the coffee shop this afternoon."

Soft pink color rose to Lorna's cheeks.

"Guilty," Mack said, before she had to respond. "But why would anyone care about that?"

"Haven't you ever lived in a small town?" Maisie asked. "That's *exactly* the kind of thing *everyone* cares about."

"And also," Dodge said. "I was at the feed store this morning and someone mentioned seeing a white truck driving through this neighborhood several times last night. They thought someone was trying to case the place to rob everyone."

"Ah shit. I hadn't thought about that," Mack said, offering Lorna a one-shouldered shrug. "I did drive by your house a few times last night. But I was just worried about you and the kids, and that Lyle might come back after I'd left."

"Yeah, so, Lyle Williams is the other reason we're here," Maisie said. "He was in the library this afternoon using our computers, and I heard him asking one of the other librarians all these questions about different commercial businesses in town and what was involved in transferring ownership of a business. He didn't come right out and mention the coffee shop by name, but from what I overheard, that's what he was interested in finding out about."

Lorna's face drained of color, and she sank into the corner of the sofa next to where Mack stood. He eased himself down onto the edge, wanting to take her hand, but settled for pressing the side of his leg to hers.

"I knew it," she said. "He's coming after the shop. I think he wanted this house. He strolled in here last night like he already owned the place. Literally just let himself into *my* house. But when I told him it still belonged to my mom, he must have started digging into if I owned the building downtown."

"The nerve of that guy," Maisie said.

"Something must have happened with Misty. Otherwise, he wouldn't be back in town." Lorna looked at Dodge. "Have you heard about her or anything about why he's back?"

Dodge shook his head. "I hadn't heard he was in town at all until tonight when I told Maisie that I'd overheard the talk at the diner about you two hooking up."

"We haven't 'hooked up'," Lorna said. "But I may have given Lyle the impression that we're a couple."

"And a few people at the coffee shop today may have overheard him calling me her boyfriend when he dropped in for a visit," Mack explained. "Although I have a feeling that's the only reason he left, both last night and this afternoon."

"Then you'd better keep it up," Maisie said. "I know you were married to him, Lorna, but I've never liked that guy. There's something a little scary about him. And I think you're better off with him thinking a big strong cowboy is with you and the kids. In fact, I think you should make sure *everyone* in town thinks you're a couple, just in case he starts asking around about you two."

"How do you suggest we do that?" Mack asked, not that he was opposed to the idea. He nudged Lorna's knee, trying to get her to smile. "Maybe another make-out session? But this time in town square, maybe on the courthouse lawn?"

She nudged him back, a tiny smile tugging at the corners of her lips before turning to Maisie. "Any other suggestions?"

"I don't know," Dodge said, scrubbing a hand over his jaw. "More PDA might be just what you need to convince this guy he isn't needed *or wanted* around you."

Lorna shook her head. "I am *not* making out with your brother on the courthouse lawn."

Dodge laughed. "I didn't mean that. But maybe a smaller public display of affection like holding hands or just being seen together in town."

"You two should go out to dinner together, like at The Tipsy Pig," Maisie suggested, naming the most popular barbeque place in town. "Dodge and I can watch the kids. But you should do it soon. Like tomorrow. And go when the most people will see you. And then maybe get some ice cream afterwards and hold hands while you walk down Main Street. Nothing says a real couple like holding hands while eating ice cream. Every romance novel will attest to that."

Mack looked at Lorna. "What do you think?"

She shrugged. "It makes a certain kind of sense.

Although I don't want to give Lyle any more reason to get angry."

Fury lit in Mack's gut. He hated that her first thoughts went to not making the guy mad. And hated it even more that she even *had* to worry about his temper. "We wouldn't be goading him or flaunting anything in his face. I think what Dodge and Maisie are suggesting is that if we're seen by enough people around town as a couple, then word will organically get back to Lyle."

Dodge nodded. "And it'll give you credibility if the guy starts asking around about you."

Mack picked up Lorna's hand and gave it a squeeze. "Look, I'm already being talked about in this town, so it doesn't bother me to be part of someone's gossip, but I understand if you're cautious about people thinking we're together. Although I'd sure rather have folks talking about how the new guy got such a gorgeous girl to go out with him than for being another one of Brandy Lassiter's bastard sons."

Lorna frowned. "Stop. That doesn't matter to me. I would be proud for people to think I'm with you."

Her words hit him square in the heart. 'Proud' wasn't normally a word people used when it came to him. It made him want to prove he was worthy of her pride.

"Thank you," he said softly, just to her.

Maisie clapped her hands together. "Sounds like we have a plan. Tipsy Pig, tomorrow night, say around six. Do you want to drop the kids off at my place, or should I pick them up?"

"I can drop them off," Lorna said. "Are you sure you're okay keeping them? They can be a handful."

Maisie nodded. "Of course. Dodge will help me, and we'll have fun with them. In fact, why don't you bring their pajamas, and they can just sleep over. Give you a break for the night."

Lorna offered Mack a tiny shrug. "I guess we're going on a date."

After working out the details, Maisie and Dodge left, and Mack cleaned up the checkers while Lorna put Max to bed.

"He was practically asleep by the time his head hit the pillow." She stifled a yawn. "He was plum wore out."

"Seems like he's not the only one," Mack said, tossing the last of the toys he'd been picking up into the bin. "I'd better get out of here and let you get to bed. But I'll see you in the morning at the coffee shop. Seven again?"

"That would be great," she said, following him to the front door. "It seems like a lot though, now you're not just helping me at the shop, but also taking me on a fake date. You sure you're okay doing this?"

He turned to face her. "I'm more than okay. With all of it. I told you I'd do anything to help you."

"I just don't want to cause you any problems. Or put you on Lyle's radar."

Mack huffed. "I can handle Lyle. In fact, I'd almost welcome the guy to come at me. I've wanted to deck him from the minute he walked into this house."

She nodded. "I get it."

"I do see one problem with this plan though," he told her.

"What's that?"

"If we're going to try to convince people we're a

real couple..." he said, offering her a roguish grin as he slid one arm around her waist and pulled her close. "I think we might need to practice some of that PDA my brother was talking about."

A smile played at the corner of her lips as she placed her hand on his chest. "Oh yeah?"

"I mean, it makes sense. I don't want to try to kiss you while we're out somewhere and have our noses bump or have it seem awkward." He reached his hand up to cup her cheek and grazed his thumb along her bottom lip. "So, it only makes sense that we do a few practice runs before tomorrow night."

"Yes. That does make sense." Her words came out breathy, and he caught the slightest tremble in her voice.

But he remembered her reaction from earlier that afternoon and wanted to take it slow.

He leaned in closer but paused right before his lips met hers. "So, Lorna, is it okay if I kiss you?"

Her fingers clutched the fabric of his shirt in her hand as she breathed out one word. "Yes."

Slowly, softly, he grazed her lips with his, savoring her quick inhale then capturing her breath as it released with a soft kiss. He kissed her mouth again, keeping it tender and slow, then pressed a gentle kiss to her cheek, then another along her jaw, and another on her neck.

She smelled like her perfume mixed with baby shampoo and tasted like spearmint gum. The wide collar of her sweatshirt had slipped down over her shoulder, and he could finally run his lips over the bare skin that he'd been fantasizing about all night.

She dropped her head back, giving him permission

to sample more of her as she let out a quiet moan, and he had to hold himself back from pressing her against the door and ripping those snug leggings off.

But he used every ounce of control he could muster and kept his hands from roaming over her curves.

Just being able to kiss her was enough.

For now.

Back at her mouth, he played his lips against hers, drawing her in then deepening the kiss.

It took everything he had to finally pull away.

Still holding onto his shirt, she stared up at him, looking a little dazed and breathless. "Wow," she whispered.

"Yeah." Putting his hat on, he took a step back and opened the door. "I think we've almost got the hang of it," he said, offering her another grin. "But I think we'd better practice some more tomorrow."

Practice makes perfect.

Chapter Fourteen

LORNA DREW IN a deep breath as Mack pulled his truck into the parking lot of the Tipsy Pig the following night.

"We're here," he announced a little too loudly, and she wondered if he was half as nervous as she was.

She'd spent close to an hour that afternoon destroying her closet as she tried to find something to wear. Shorts seemed too casual, and the only jeans that fit were the two pair she wore to the coffee shop, and she didn't really want to wear her *work jeans* on a date—even if it was a pretend one.

Even though Izzy was almost a year old, she still hadn't taken off all the baby weight and her body seemed to have changed after having a second child, so half the stuff she tried on was either too small or didn't look right on her anymore.

Not for the first, or what seemed like the hundredth time this week, she'd wished Leni had been there. They'd spent so many years apart with her older sister in college at MIT and building her career in aerospace engineering, but having her back in Woodland Hills for most of the past year and living in their old house together had been so fun, and she'd come to depend on the support and friendship of her sister again.

Although, knowing Leni, she probably would have created a spreadsheet of outfit choices, a list of pros and cons for each one, and reorganized her closet while they were at it.

It was killing her not to text or call to tell her about Lyle being back—and about kissing Mack—and talking through what she should do about both things. But her sister deserved this honeymoon, and she didn't want to do anything to spoil her and Chevy's time together. And knowing the two of them, if they sensed trouble at home, they'd pack up and be on the first plane back to Colorado.

No, she was an adult. She just needed to pull up her big girl panties and face going out on a fake date with a hot cowboy on her own.

She twisted the strap of her purse around her fist as she peered across the parking lot, trying to see if she recognized any of the cars.

"You okay?" Mack asked, nodding to her knee, which had been shaking for the past five minutes. "You're as fidgety as a long-tailed cat in a room full of rocking chairs."

"Yes, I'm fine," she said, pressing her foot into the floor of the truck to stop it from shaking. "It's just that...well...I got married not long after high school, and this last year my focus has been on the kids...and it just feels a little pathetic that this is the first date I've been on in eight years. *And* it isn't even real." She wrapped the strap tighter until it suddenly gave way and snapped apart in her hands. "Oh shoot."

Tears threatened as she stared down at the two torn pieces.

"Hey, now," Mack said, sliding an arm around her shoulder and pulling her to him. "We don't have to do this. The last thing I want to think is that going out on a date with me makes you cry."

She shook her head against his shoulder and huffed out a small laugh. "It's not you. You're amazing..."

"And so damn hot, if I recall the words you used yesterday," he said, obviously trying to tease a smile out of her.

She laughed again. "Yes, and so damn hot that any girl would be lucky to go out with you." She blew out a breath. "It's just been a long time. I haven't really been out on a date since high school. I don't remember how to even act."

"I get it. All those months I was in Texas, I was working so hard, and only left the ranch a few times, so it's been a dang long time since I've been out on a date, as well. But I can honestly say, you're the only woman I've *wanted* to take on a date in years, even if it is a fake one."

"That's sweet, but I'm not sure that takes the pressure off."

He chuckled. "There's no pressure. And I'm serious, we don't have to do this at all. If this makes you uncomfortable, I'm happy to take you home. We can pick up a pizza on the way."

The idea of going home, putting on comfy pants, and scarfing down a pizza did sound appealing.

She lifted her chin. "No. I can do this. I'm just being silly. Lyle always said I tended to be overdramatic."

Mack's easy expression darkened. "First of all, you

need to stop giving two shits about what Lyle said about anything. That guy is a fool and an idiot and a few other choice words that I probably shouldn't say in front of a lady. You're *not* being silly. *Or* overdramatic. You're being honest. And real. And you have every right to feel *whatever* you're feeling."

"Thank you," she whispered around the sudden lump in her throat. Apparently, there *were* still good men left in this world.

And if she could just get over herself, she could go out on a fake date with one of them.

"There's one thing I know I can make better." He reached over the seat, dug through a tool pouch, and came back with a small coil of thin wire in his hand and a pair of pliers. "Hand me your purse. It won't be perfect, but there's not much either bailing wire or duct tape can't fix."

She laughed as she handed over her bag. "It's an old purse anyway. So, anything you can do to hold it together until I get home will be great. I just wanted something smaller than my normal gigantic purse slash tote slash diaper bag."

The purse, which now that she thought about it, was in the back of her closet because the strap had already been a little bit torn, had broken on the side with the buckle. Mack undid the buckle and tossed the broken section to the floor of the pickup, then poked the wire through the hole on the good part of the strap and looped it through the small ring on the side of the purse. Twisting the pieces of wire together, he cut off the excess and tucked the sharp edge and the remains of the torn strap into the bag.

"It's not perfect, but it should do what you need it

to." He offered her a gentle smile as he handed back the mended purse. "Kind of like this date. If you still want to go on it…"

She smiled back as she nodded. "I do."

His face broke into a happy grin. "Stay right there," he said then got out of the truck and hurried around to open her door. He held out his hand to help her climb from the cab.

She'd finally settled on a flouncy light blue dress that hit her mid-thigh and had a wide, open neckline, a lower cut in the back, and small flutter sleeves. Digging out her curling iron, she'd even spent extra time creating big wavy curls that cascaded over her shoulders and back. She'd found a pair of navy-blue wedge-heeled sandals that she hadn't worn in years and had even painted her toenails a bright watermelon pink.

By the time she'd left the house, she felt like a real person again for the first time in a long time, not just someone's mom, and she had a smidge of confidence in the way she looked.

Mack, on the other hand, looked good enough to eat in faded jeans, his normal square-toed cowboy boots, his gray felt cowboy hat, and a fitted black snap-up western shirt that hugged his broad shoulders and had her thinking all sorts of naughty thoughts about yanking open those snaps and running her tongue over those rock hard abs he'd been flaunting the other day in the barn.

He placed his arm around her as they walked across the parking lot, and she inhaled the scent of him. His cologne was a mix of something woodsy, soft citrus, and sandalwood and threatened to send her into a swoon.

He leaned closer to her ear as they approached the restaurant door. "And just for the record, I think you're pretty damn hot, too. Especially in that dress."

A smile curved her lips. If she wasn't careful, she could really fall for Mack Lassiter.

Or maybe she already had.

The hostess had sat them at a table by the window with a great view of the mountains, and things were going fine until Lorna spilled her water and it poured right into Mack's lap. The guy seemed unfazed as he laughed it off, sopped it up with the extra napkins on the table, and signaled for the hostess to bring her another water.

"It feels like everyone is already staring at us," she whispered. "Now I've drawn even more attention by being such a klutz. We're supposed to be an established couple, but I don't know how to stop acting like a nervous girl on a first date."

"Don't worry about it," Mack said, reaching across the table to hold her hand. "We just need to think about how two people who really *were* a couple would act."

She looked around the restaurant and nodded to a man and woman in their mid-forties who went to her church. "Well, the Nelsons have been married for like twenty years, so they're a real couple, and they're just ignoring each other and looking at their phones."

Mack laughed. "I'm not sure that's the best route to take. I don't want you to seem bored with me already. How about instead, we stare into each other's eyes and act like whatever we're talking about is the most interesting conversation in the world?"

She let out a soft chuckle. He had an easy way of making her laugh. "I can do that."

"And I'll call you a cute pet name when the waitress comes back if you act like my conversation skills are so fascinating and witty that you can't look away."

She caught the waitress, a woman named Luciana, who'd been a few years ahead of her in school and usually ordered a Caramel Macchiato when she came into the coffee shop, approaching and let out a hearty laugh.

"Oh Mack, you tell the funniest stories," she said, probably a bit too loudly.

"Thanks Sugar Muffin," Mack said sweetly, then acted startled as the waitress appeared at his elbow.

"Hey Lorna, you two seem like you're having a good time over here. But I'm not sure I've met your friend," Lucianna said, glancing at Mack.

"You mean my *boyfriend*?" Lorna asked and tried not to wince at how stupidly cringy that had sounded. "This is Mack Lassiter."

"Oh sure, you're Ford's brother. I mean, I know you're Dodge and Chevy's brother, too. But Ford and I were in the same class in high school. We were lab partners for Chemistry our senior year, and he used to bribe me with Snickers to take all the notes." She pointed a well-manicured fingernail at Mack. "I think I did meet you sometime last year."

Mack nodded. "I was here last fall. That's when I

met Lorna. Then I had to go back to Texas to help out on the ranch where I used to work." He offered what felt like a meaningful look at Lorna. "But I'm here for good now."

She waved her pen between them. "And now you two are dating?"

"Well, it started last fall. I think I fell for her the first day we met, back when I was here the first time," he explained. "I mean look at her, she's gorgeous. Totally out of my league. My family helped hers at the Beans and Brews festival, but the chili wasn't the only thing there that I thought was hot. Then after I left, we had kind of a long-distance thing, and I won her over. And now that I'm back, we're all in. Totally a couple."

He winced at Lorna as if he realized that he'd given way too much backstory.

Real smooth, Lassiter. Totally natural.

"Oh-kay. Thank you for that detailed explanation," Luciana said, then grinned at Lorna. "He's cute, but a little nerdy, huh?"

Lorna laughed. "Yes, to both."

The waitress laughed with her then tapped her pen to her notepad. "So, what'll you have, Sugar Muffin?"

Chapter Fifteen

THEIR DATE HAD started out rocky, but Lorna felt like things smoothed out after their food arrived and they had something else to concentrate on. Although, getting the baby back ribs might not have been the best choice since she ended up with a mortifyingly ridiculous amount of barbeque sauce on her face.

But instead of being grossed out or humiliated like Lyle would have acted, Mack just laughed it off and slid one of his ribs across his cheek to match hers.

They talked all through the meal *and* while they walked along Main Street eating ice cream and holding hands, as Maisie had instructed. She learned about the ranch where he'd been working, and he seemed genuinely interested in funny stories about Max as a toddler, what a hard time she was having getting Izzy to eat fruit, and the marketing ideas she had for the coffee shop.

For as much as they'd been talking nonstop for the past two hours, Mack was surprisingly quiet now as he walked her to her front door.

"I really had fun tonight," she said, suddenly feeling

like this date—and the awkwardness of deciding to kiss him goodnight or invite him in—was all too real.

"Me too." He stuffed his hands into the front pockets of his jeans. She wasn't sure if that was to show he wasn't going to try a move on her or to keep himself from touching her.

She wasn't sure if she was happy with either option.

That kiss the night before—and the one in the alley—had shaken her to her core. The passion and intensity they'd generated—in that first kiss alone—had heat flooding through her body and in places that hadn't felt heat like that in a long time.

She couldn't remember *ever* being kissed like that before.

And just looking at him now and wondering—*hoping*—if he might kiss her again, had her chest and face flushing like a furnace had been turned on inside her.

There were a million reasons why she should tell him 'thank you and goodnight' and send him back to his truck, the greatest being that her crazy, *and dangerous*, ex was back in town, and she had no idea what he was going to do when he heard people talking about her and Mack holding hands on Main Street. But also, because she was a single mom and a business owner who didn't have time in her life for a relationship.

Or the strength of heart to fall in love and then trust that another man wouldn't leave her again.

And those were just in the top five. There were other reasons to not invite this man inside, like not letting her kids get attached to someone else who might leave.

But there was one wild and reckless and completely unreasonable reason to open the door that seemed to outweigh all the smart, sensible ones.

She wanted this man.

With every fiber in her being.

She didn't do reckless. Her first choice was usually comfortable shoes, and she made practical 'mom decisions' like using coupons at the grocery store and encouraging Max to eat broccoli and take swimming lessons.

But tonight was not about being a mom. It was about being a woman. A woman with needs and desires.

"Do you want to come in?" The words came out more quietly than she'd meant them to.

She watched his Adams apple bob as he swallowed, then he nodded slowly, as if he understood just what she was asking when she invited him inside.

They'd barely shut the door when she reached for him, pulling him close, then his mouth captured hers.

The kiss was deep and demanding as his hands roamed over her body, exploring her curves.

This wasn't part of their pretend relationship or practicing their PDA. This was all raw emotion and sizzling heat, and a need for this man that overwhelmed all else.

Finally able to do the thing she'd been fantasizing about all night, she gripped the front of his shirt and tore the snaps open then bent her head to kiss the hard muscled chest she'd unwrapped.

"Take me upstairs," she practically panted in his ear.

He paused long enough to pull off his cowboy boots and shrug out of his shirt, then he bent and swooped her up, cradling her body against his bare chest as he carried her upstairs and into her bedroom. She kicked off her sandals as he set her on the bed then pulled her dress over her head, tossed it to the floor and scooted back to give him room to join her.

For as long as it had taken her to choose the dress, she'd given little thought to her underwear, not anticipating that anyone would see it, and she'd worn her normal black bikini panties and a black underwire bra.

Mack seemed to appreciate them anyway, and a small smile played at the corners of his lips as his gaze raked over her. "Not that you'd hear me complain, but I'm awful glad you're not wearing those same undies you had on at the wedding."

She laughed. "Those were my spanx—they were for special occasion dresses. This is what you get on a normal Tuesday."

"Tuesday just became my favorite day of the week," he said, shucking off his jeans and crawling onto the bed in a pair of black boxer briefs. "I don't care what kind of underwear you're wearing, because darlin', as far as I'm concerned, you won't be wearing them long enough for me to even notice."

It took him about two seconds to get her naked, and the look in his eyes as his gaze raked over her body sent heat rushing through every part of her. It was addictive—the pure desire he had for her, and she surprised herself with the brazen way she let him look.

Then touch.

His big hands covered her breasts, and she bit back a moan as his thumb grazed over the pebbled nub of one of her nipples. He bent his head, and she couldn't hold back the next moan as he circled the tip with his tongue then drew it between his lips.

His mouth was warm, and the things he was doing with his tongue were sending surges of heat to her very core, like the string vibrating between two plastic telephone cups, except he was communicating in a new and exciting way.

He took his time, touching and caressing as he savored and sampled her, discovering what she liked and what made her squirm. He tantalized and teased, and every touch, every lick, every caress of his hands and his lips sent pleasure coursing through her, and she arched her back, willing him to take more.

Planting a trail of kisses along her belly, he moved lower, his breath warm on her most sensitive spot as he spread her legs then bent his head to taste and sample more. The scrape of his whiskers against the sensitive areas of her thighs had her wanting to cry out.

She let out a tiny moan, thinking she had to be quiet, than realized they were alone in the house, so there was no need to be quiet or to try to hold back. Something in her, some feral and wanton part of her, just wanted to let go, to feel, to give, to take, to let herself experience the pure sensual heat of this man's head between her legs and the delicious things he was doing with his tongue.

The scrape of his teeth, the soft tug of his lips, sent desire straight to her core, and she surrendered to the pure pleasure of it.

She felt like she was drowning in him, but she didn't want to be saved. She was lost in him, enraptured by the feel of his hands, his mouth, and the coil of heat building inside her.

She'd almost forgotten this feeling, this sensation of pure pleasure, and she abandoned herself to it, crying out as the exquisite waves of pleasure rocked through her.

She lay breathless, too many sensations happening at once as he rose above her. The pleasure he'd given her only seemed to amplify his own enjoyment, and she loved the way he looked at her, as if she were a prize that he couldn't quite believe he'd won.

"You are so beautiful," he whispered in her ear before he leaned over the bed, wrenching his wallet from the pocket of his jeans and extracting a foil packet. Covering himself, he settled in between her legs, then paused as he peered down at her. "Are you sure this is what you want?"

"I cannot think of anything in my life that I have wanted more."

He growled in response as he entered her, holding her gaze as he set the pace, starting slowly then giving her more. And more.

She matched his rhythm, her body all nerve endings and sensation, heat surging through her as she gave in to desire and savored the sweet torment as he took her closer and closer to the edge again.

But there was something more happening, something beyond the pleasure and the sweet nothings he whispered into her ear, and for just this moment, this one night, she let herself go, let her trust this man with not just her body, but her heart.

She may regret it in the morning, but for right now, she could only cling to him, giving him everything she had, surrendering to him and crying out as he pulled her close, his grip on her tightening as his muscles constricted. His teeth scraped against her shoulder, and a growl tore from his throat as he tensed and shuddered, matching her release with his own.

Then he fell onto the tangled sheets next to her and drew her to him. She wrapped her body around his as he pressed a kiss to her forehead.

She snuggled into him, relishing the feel of his exquisitely muscled body, and thinking that for two people who were starting a fake relationship, their first date had ended in a way that was all too real.

But those thoughts were for tomorrow. For tonight, she was going to let go and enjoy this man, again. And again.

Chapter Sixteen

"YOU GOT THIS, Dylan," Mack called out to the boy the next day. "You're doing great."

He and Judy stood just inside the fence as they watched the boy lead the pony in a slow circle around the corral.

"Look at that smile," Judy said. "He loves this."

"Duke told me that mare turned twenty this year, so she doesn't get ridden much anymore, but she's doing great with Dylan."

Judy nudged his arm. "Us old gals can still have a little spunk left in us."

"Come on, Miss Judy. What would you know about being old?"

A hearty laugh burst from her. "You definitely inherited the Lassiter charm. But I'm feeling every one of my years today. Raising a grandson in your sixties is not for the faint of heart."

"Seems to me like you're doing a great job with him. And you scored major grandma points by bringing him out here today." Mack couldn't imagine his mother *ever* treating him to a special outing like this, let alone taking him out of school for it. He pointed at Dylan, who was giggling as the horse broke into a trot. "He's really getting the hang of it. Might just turn out to be a cowboy yet. Although that astronaut thing should probably still be considered as a contender."

"I'm sure he'll keep it in mind. He's also tossed around fireman and furniture salesman. He's a fan of our recliners and thinks it would be nice to get a discount on the next ones we buy."

Mack laughed. "Smart kid. And thankfully, he's got plenty of time to decide."

"I notice that my grandson isn't the only one who can't stop smiling today," she said, her lips quirking up in a teasing grin. "You seem to be in a pretty good mood, too."

He gave her what he hoped looked like an innocent shrug. "Yeah, I guess I am."

"Does this good mood have anything to do with the date I heard you were on last night with a certain pretty coffee shop owner?"

He grinned. "Yes, it just might. But how did you hear I took Lorna on a date last night?"

Judy chuckled. "Oh honey. Of course I heard. This is a *very* small town. And apparently you were holding hands and walking right down Main Street."

Maisie was right. And it seemed like their plan had worked. People were already talking about them as a couple.

Hopefully Lyle had heard about them as well.

"I ran into her at the grocery store this morning, and she seemed pretty happy, too," Judy said. "It's nice to see her smiling again. Especially after what that douche-hole Lyle Williams put her through."

Just thinking about Lyle had Mack's temper flare, and he curled his hands into fists. He took a deep breath and tried to let his rage out with his exhale. "I haven't heard that particular terminology, but I'd agree it seems fitting."

"I don't know a lot about their marriage," Judy said. "But I know enough to tell you that Lyle is bad news, and there is nothing good about him being back in town. A lot of people felt bad for Lorna when he took off on her, but I was glad to see him go. And I wasn't the only one." She shook her head and wrinkled her nose as if she'd just gotten a whiff of cow manure. "I can't imagine why that sweet Misty would give up everything and leave town with him. And I honestly can't believe he's back. I'm not one to gossip, but I think he left owing money to more than one person in this town, and I can't imagine he found that much while they've been gone."

"I agree on the bad news. And it seems to me that the best thing Lyle ever did for Lorna was to leave her."

Judy brushed a hand over his shoulder. "I'm glad she has you now."

"Thanks. I'd like to make her happy, but sometimes I'm not sure I'm the right guy for her." He wasn't sure why he'd just admitted that to someone who was practically a stranger, especially since the whole plan was to make them seem like an established blissful couple. But the older woman was easy to talk to, and the words had just come out.

Her brow furrowed. "What do you mean?"

He looked down and kicked at a clod of dirt with the toe of his boot. "I like Lorna. A lot. But I'm not sure I know how to do this whole serious dating thing. I'm not sure what Duke's told you about my past, but my dad was never around and even when my mom was home, she might as well have been gone too, because she could care less about me or what I was doing." He stared out over the mountains behind the corral. "I want to be a good boyfriend, but what do I know about how to have a healthy relationship?"

"Well, it sounds like you sure know what an *unhealthy* one looks like."

"I do."

"So, just do the opposite of that."

He huffed out a laugh. "Good advice. Although I have to say I expected something more from someone who's older and wiser, such as yourself."

"Aw hell. What do I know? Being older doesn't always make you smarter. Sometimes it just makes you older." She laughed at herself. "But I do know plenty of people who came from broken homes and crappy lives who are wonderful partners in marriage."

"Yeah, I guess." His brothers had also been abandoned by their mother, and they all three seemed to be good guys and to be in strong relationships.

"I wasn't just being a smart ass when I said that you know what *not* to do. Loving someone means showing up and being there and listening and doing your best to take care of them. I was married for forty years before that bastard cancer took my husband, and I can tell you that relationships aren't always easy. They take work and commitment. But dadgumit, if you find your person, the one who makes you happy, who you can't imagine living your life without, and who you want to do that work for, they sure are worth it."

He nodded but wasn't sure how to respond.

"And don't assume just because you had shitty parents, you aren't still worthy of being loved." She held his gaze. "I understand a little about your situation and your mom. My daughter is an addict, too. I love her, but she has a disease, and she doesn't know how to overcome that disease enough to focus on being a mom. But I'm thankful every dang day for the chance I have to be with my grandson. It's not always easy, but I'm so glad I get to watch him grow up and be here for him. I love that boy more than I could ever imagine." She jerked her thumb back toward the ranch house. "Your grandfather loves you the same way."

Mack frowned. "I might be growing on him, but I can't imagine he feels anything like what you're describing."

"Why not?"

He shrugged, uncomfortable now with the focus being on him and how his grandfather felt about him. "He barely knows me."

"Oh, honey. You're wrong. You are a child of his child. He loved you from the moment you came into existence. I can promise you that. I think he's so glad for the chance to get to know you now and to make up for all that time you two lost." She nudged his shoulder. "And don't sell yourself short. You seem like a pretty lovable guy. I imagine Lorna sees that. Now you just have to *let* yourself be loved."

"Thanks Judy. You're a good grandma."

"Anytime. I knew your grandma, and June Lassiter

was a pretty amazing woman. I think she would have told you the same thing." She sighed. "I wish you would have had a chance to know her."

"Me, too."

She glanced down at her watch. "Shoot. I've got to get back to the office. But this has been fun, for Dylan, and for me."

He called for the boy to bring the horse over then gave him a quick lesson on how to remove her saddle and blanket and brush down her coat. They made a plan for him to come out again the next week, then Mack waved goodbye as they hurried toward Judy's Subaru.

His phone buzzed as he was giving the mare a handful of oats and praising her for a job well done that day. He pulled it from his pocket and smiled at Lorna's name on the screen. He tapped to accept the call. "Hey, beautiful."

"Lyle has Max," she cried, her voice panicked and shaky. "He picked him up from school without my consent, and I don't know where he took him."

Chapter Seventeen

"Okay, slow down," Mack said, already sprinting toward his truck. "Where are you?"

"I'm driving around town looking for Lyle's black Honda."

"I'm coming." He started the engine and put the truck in gear. Gravel spit from beneath his tires as he tore down the driveway. "Hold on, I'll be to town in two minutes. I'm already on the highway. Tell me where to look. Or tell me where to meet you, and we'll look for him together."

"I don't know. I've already called my house, just in case he brought him home. But Gertie said she hadn't seen them. I've checked the diner parking lot and the drugstore thinking he might have taken him for ice cream, but didn't see his car either place. Not that he'd ever done that in all the years we were married, but I don't know what else to do." She sobbed into the phone. "What if he really took him? What if he's driving down the pass with him, and I'm just running around town thinking they went for ice cream?"

"Hang on, honey. I'm driving into town now. Where are you?"

"I just drove back to the school. Should I call the police?"

"I don't know. Maybe. Let's keep looking for a few minutes then decide." He turned into the parking lot of the school and saw her sitting in her minivan, her head bent over the steering wheel, her shoulders shaking. "I'm here."

He parked next to her and bolted from his truck. She looked up, saw him, and started crying harder as she opened her car door and fell into his arms.

He pulled her close, rubbing her back as he murmured soft words into her hair. "It's okay. Shh. I'm here. We'll find him."

She pulled back, sucked in a deep breath then swiped at the tears on her cheeks. "I'm all right. Just had to get that out of my system."

Her hands were shaking, and he picked them up and squeezed them in his. "Come on. We'll look for him together. We can take your car since you have the booster seat, but I'll drive, and you can watch for them. We can search this whole town in fifteen minutes. If we don't find them by then, we'll call the police. Deal?"

"Yes. Deal." She ran around the car to get into the passenger side as he slid behind the wheel and started the van. "Tell me again where you've already checked."

"The diner, the drugstore, my house, the fairgrounds, and the school. I feel like I've driven up and down Main Street several times and the side streets around the school."

He put the car in gear and headed out of the parking lot. "Think like a dad. Where would you want to take your son for an outing? Maybe the high school football field where Lyle used to play, or a baseball field to play catch?"

"Good idea. Let's drive by the high school. I can imagine Lyle wanting to brag about his football days, but I can't see him trying to play catch with Max." She pulled a Kleenex from a box in the console and blew her nose. It felt like she was calming down now that they had a plan.

The high school was only a few blocks away, but no cars were in the lot and the football field was empty.

"What about the park?" he asked, scanning the side streets as he drove through an intersection. "Did you check there?"

"No, but that's a good idea, too. Max loves to swing." She leaned forward to peer through the windshield as he turned onto the street with the park.

Mack caught sight of Lyle first, sitting on a bench next to the playground, his head down as he focused on his phone. Then he saw Max, his small legs straddling the bars at the top of the climbing structure. His shoulders sank inward and even from across the lawn, Mack thought it looked like he was crying.

"There he is," Lorna cried, already reaching for the door handle as Mack pulled into a parking spot. She flew out of the truck and tore across the grass, calling her son's name.

Mack raced after her, trying to keep an eye on the boy *and* his mother. *And* his asshole father.

Lyle finally looked up from his phone, saw Lorna

running toward the playground, and stood, a smirk on his face that Mack would take supreme pleasure in smacking off.

Max saw Lorna, and his face lit up. "Mommy," he called, but in his haste to try to climb off the top of the structure, his foot missed the final bar, and he fell forward, smacking his face on it before his body fell to the ground.

"Max!" Lorna sprinted to her son, Mack right on her heels.

The boy lifted his head to let out a wail of pain as bright red blood spilled from his mouth.

"Oh dang," he heard Lyle say as Mack fell to his knees in front of Lorna as she gathered Max into her arms.

"Let Mommy see," she told Max, trying to pull him back as he cried into her shoulder. "You're okay, but it looks like you split your lip, and you've got a bump on your cheek."

"I fink I bit ma tongue," Max said as he opened his mouth and blood spilled over his bottom lip.

"I've got my Stanley cup in the car. I'm sure it's still got ice in it. We can put some on your lip and cheek as we drive to the Urgent Care."

"For shit's sake, Lorna. You don't have to baby him or run off to the doctor for every little bruise." Lyle had come up behind them and was leaning casually on the side of the play structure. "It's just a split lip. Put some ice on it. It'll be fine."

Mack wondered if Lyle had used that line on her as he watched the array of emotions flash across Lorna's face—terror, sadness, anger, then pure white-hot rage.

Her son had to weigh fifty pounds, but she lifted

him as if he were a toddler, clutching him to her chest as she narrowed her eyes at Lyle and spoke with a barely contained fury. "He wouldn't *have* a split lip *or* a bloody face if you hadn't taken him from school. Without. My. Permission."

Anger flashed across Lyle's face. "I don't need your permission to see my own son."

"But you do need to watch him if he's in your care," Mack said. "What the hell was he doing on top of that jungle gym anyway?"

Lyle snapped his head up, then pushed away from the play structure and stuck his chest out toward Mack. "Who the hell are you to tell me anything about my son? Just because you're fucking my wife, that doesn't give you the right to tell me how to treat *my* kid."

"Ex-wife," Lorna spat before Mack could correct him.

Max whimpered as he buried his face in Lorna's shoulder. She hugged him closer as she took a step between the two men.

Which made Mack feel like a worthless schmuck. He was supposed to be protecting her. And he wasn't about to let this asshole hurt her, *or her kids,* ever again.

"You need to stay away from this family," Mack said through gritted teeth as he stepped to the side of Lorna. His fists were clenched at his sides, but he was just waiting for Lyle to give him a reason to use them.

"No. I don't. This is *my* family. I *own* them. They belong to me." Lyle's sneer held a mix of malice and spite. He turned to Lorna, putting his face right in front of hers. "Don't forget that, Lorna."

This time, Mack inserted his body between them,

then grabbed Lyle by the shirt collar and hauled him up to his chest. "You gave up your right to this family. Now I think it's time for you to leave before we call the cops and tell them how you took Max from school without his mother's permission. I think in this state, that's considered kidnapping."

Mack shoved him away, but he caught himself as he stumbled back. Then he held up his hands and let out a disdainful laugh. "Fine. I'm going. No need to get the cops involved. But Lorna, don't forget how easy it was for me to take my son away from you today."

Lorna clasped her hands in her lap as Mack pulled the truck up in front of the house at the ranch a few hours later. Duke had already invited them for supper, and it hadn't taken much convincing when Mack suggested they spend the night as well.

He'd been great through the whole ordeal that afternoon, dealing with Lyle then driving them to the pediatrician's office, while Lorna sat in the back with Max, holding a napkin wrapped around the ice from her cup against his lip.

The pediatrician confirmed that Max had bit his tongue and assured Lorna he didn't need stitches in his lip. He'd prescribed Children's Tylenol, rest, soft foods, and as many popsicles as Max wanted.

Lorna glanced into the back seat where both kids were sound asleep. Max had stopped taking afternoon naps years ago, but the combination of medicine, trauma, and the lull of Mack's truck engine must have done him in.

She slumped against the seat, fatigue stealing over her, and she felt wearier than she had in a long time. "Can we just sit here for a minute?"

"Sure. I'll even leave the engine running so the kids don't wake up." Mack offered her an encouraging smile as he reached over and took her hand. "He's okay, Lorn."

She nodded, tears threatening. She squeezed his hand as she swallowed them back. "I know. And he's bonked his face and hit his head before, but this is different. It's not even so much that Max got hurt while he was with Lyle, it's more about how easily that asshole walked up to the school and just took my son."

"I still can't believe they let that happen. Don't they have some kind of rules about who can pick kids up?"

"They do, but from what Max said, he was already in front of the school when Lyle came up to him and said I'd asked him to pick him up. There are teachers and admins there who have either known Lyle forever or just know he's Max's dad from when he was in preschool there last year." She looked out across the farmyard as she shook her head. "And honestly, because Lyle was gone, I'm not sure if I ever took his name off the list of approved people to pick Max up from school. How could I have been so stupid?"

"Hey. You're not stupid for thinking you can trust the father of your children not to hurt them."

"I am if their father is Lyle Williams." She turned back to Mack but couldn't meet his eye. She stared into her lap, summoning the courage to tell him the deepest secret and shame of her life.

Glancing in the back seat once more to make sure that Max was still asleep, she took a deep breath then in a soft voice admitted, "He used to hurt me." She shifted her gaze back to Mack, but he didn't look horrified or judgmental. Or even surprised. He just looked like Mack—his expression open and ready to listen. "That's the first time I've said it out loud, to anyone. I'm ashamed to admit it, but Lyle used to hit me."

His expression changed now as his brow furrowed. "You have nothing to be ashamed of. He's the only one who's at fault here."

"That's kind of you to say. But I'm not sure that's true. I'm still not sure how it happened. He'd seemed like such a great guy. We hadn't been dating that long, and we were always careful, but I got pregnant anyway. He seemed so excited and asked me to marry him the night I told him. I thought he really loved me. Although, as I look back now, there were probably signs that I'd missed. A hard pinch to the back of my arm when I'd said something in front of someone that embarrassed him, a playful slap on the thigh that wasn't always so playful." She shook her head. "I had no idea when I met him that he had such a capacity for anger. And not just anger, but meanness. I think someone probably hurt him when he was young."

She held up her free hand to stop him when Mack started to say something.

"I'm not excusing his behavior. But maybe that's why I did back then. I felt sorry for him. And it started slowly. The first time was a slap. And then he felt so bad and apologized so profusely. He brought me flowers and gifts and seemed like that sweet guy who I'd originally fallen for. I believed him when he said it would never happen again. And it didn't, not for a long time. And then again, not for a long time again after the next slap. We were broke and had a baby, and I was just trying to survive life, so maybe I didn't even realize what was going on until it was too late."

Mack was still holding her hand. His voice was soft as he said, "You can't blame yourself."

"It's hard not to. Especially now when I look back and see how he so methodically manipulated me. He'd always been possessive. But he made it seem like he wanted to be with me instead of that he was discouraging me from spending time with my mom or my sister or the few friends I'd had left from high school. I was kind of an introvert anyway, and in the beginning, he made me feel special the way he love-bombed me and said he wanted me all to himself and how I was the only person he needed. It wasn't until later that I realized he'd been systematically isolating me from my family and friends for years."

"That's what they do," Mack said. "My mom was with men like that. And they always made her feel like it was her fault for making them smack her. But it wasn't her fault. And it wasn't your fault either."

She shrugged, but kept a tight hold of his hand, as if it were the only thing holding her together.

"I hear women talk about it sometimes, and they always say how they would leave immediately if a man *ever* laid his hands on them. But it's not that easy. Not when you have a baby, and no money, no job, no friends, and a strained relationship with your family. And he was so kind and loving to me for months after it happened that it almost seemed worth the pain to have that sweet guy back. But, as you can imagine, things got worse, and the slaps turned into punches and the beatings got worse. I knew I was in trouble, but I didn't know how to get help."

"And your mom never knew?" Mack asked.

"Maybe. I think she suspected something wasn't right. But, like I said, I didn't see her very often, and I spent so much time at home that it was easy to hide a black eye or a bruised cheek, or a sprained wrist. The only one who ever saw the evidence was Max, and I just prayed he was too young to understand what was going on."

"Did he hurt Max?"

"No. Not physically. He said mean things, but he never hit him. But I saw it coming. His rage was escalating. He wasn't doing well at the insurance agency, and he kept borrowing money, not just from the bank here, but from a credit union in Denver, and from people in town who used to be his friends. I don't know how much he owed, but I found some of the paperwork from the bank, and it was a lot."

She glanced in the back seat again to make sure Max was still sleeping and waited to speak until she saw the rhythmic rise and fall of his small chest. "And then one night, he came home, drunk and angry at the world, and he took all that mad out on me. He beat the hell out of me. He left me on the floor in the corner of our bedroom, and when he went to the kitchen for another beer, I got Max and locked us in the bathroom all night. In the morning, I heard his car drive away and even though I had one eye so swollen shut I could barely see, I got myself to the emergency room. He'd broken my arm, and I needed stitches for a cut on my forehead. They asked if someone had hurt me, if I felt safe at home—what a joke—and if I wanted them to call the police. But I knew Lyle was going to be pissed off enough that I'd even gone to the hospital, so I lied and said that I'd fallen down the stairs."

Mack winced and squeezed her hand even harder. "I'm so sorry that happened to you."

"Me, too. And I'm sorry I didn't ask for help sooner. I'd like to think I would have, especially after that last time, but then something changed. Lyle started spending more time at the office, and then he had all these meetings he had to attend at night after work, and then a couple of out-of-town trips for some insurance conferences. I think I knew what was happening, but I didn't care. He was in a better mood, and I was just happy he was gone all the time and was leaving me alone. Everyone in town felt so sorry for me when he left town and divorced me for Misty, but they should've been feeling sorry for her."

"Do you think he tried something with Misty, and she kicked him out?"

"Maybe. Honestly, I'm a little worried about her. She's younger than me, but she grew up with three older brothers so maybe she's stronger or better at fighting back and could hold her own against Lyle. I was weak and never knew quite how to stick up for myself."

"You're not weak. You're one of the strongest

women I know. Look at all you've done in the past year and a half that he's been gone."

"Thank you. I feel stronger. Now. And like a veil has lifted, and I can finally see what was happening. I have Leni and my mom back in my life, and friends for the first time in a long time. It's a hard thing to talk about and for people to understand. I hear so many women say they would *never* let this happen to them or that they would fight back. But the women who say that aren't usually the ones who have taken a punch to the face. The pain and the shock—it stuns you, and even if you swear that the next time you're going to fight back, you can still end up cowering in the corner praying he doesn't hit you again or he's through with you for the night."

Mack still held her hand, and he pulled her from her seat and into his lap. Her shoulders were against the window and his arm was wrapped around her waist as he cradled her against him. "First of all, I want you to know that I'm proud of you."

She scoffed, but he shook his head.

"Don't do that. Don't downplay what you've survived and what you've made of your life and your children's lives. They are happy and healthy, and you're an amazing mom who puts her family first but also runs a successful business. Which you set up and started *all on your own*. That's impressive and something to be proud of."

She nodded, the emotion burning her throat again.

"And secondly, I want you to know that he will *never* touch you again. Above all else that's going on with us, I *am* your friend, and I will be here for you, no matter what. You have a family now, not just me, but the whole damn Lassiter clan, and we will never let anyone take you away or isolate you from us."

Her eyes brimmed with tears as she nodded again, unable to speak.

He held her gaze, his eyes suddenly steely and hard. "And if he *ever* hurts you or the kids again, I *will* kill him."

Chapter Eighteen

MACK'S THREAT SHOULD have scared Lorna, but all she felt was protected and cherished by this man. For the first time in so long, it seemed like she truly had a man in her corner and that Mack genuinely cared about her and her kid's well-being.

Sitting on Mack's lap, in the tight circle of his arms, with the warm spring air wafting through the open windows, she felt safe.

She wasn't looking for a hero. In fact, she'd spent the last year trying to be her own hero for her kids, and for herself.

But it felt good to feel like she had someone to count on. She'd seen Mack with her babies and with animals on the ranch, and she knew that he had a kindness and a gentleness to him that she'd never seen in Lyle. Mack Lassiter was a good man.

She leaned in and pressed a soft kiss to his mouth. The tightness in his shoulders eased and the arm around her waist pulled her closer as she kissed him again. Then again.

Everything else fell away. The only thing that mattered was this man and his mouth on hers. His free hand came up to cup her cheek, holding her face as his tongue slipped between her lips.

Heat rushed through her body, filling her with warmth and need, and she melted into him.

"Hey, if you guys are swapping gum, can I have some?" a small voice said from the back of the truck.

Mack chuckled against her mouth, and she loved the feeling of it. She'd never experienced that with Lyle. After they got married, it seemed like he'd never laughed at all.

"We're *not* swapping gum," Lorna told her son. "That's gross, Max."

"Why?" Max asked. "Gum is great."

Mack stretched his long arm along the back of the seat as he turned to grin at the boy. "Gum *is* great. But we were just kissing."

"Kissing?" Max made a barfing sound. "Now that's gross."

Their laughter filled the cab of the truck, and Lorna breathed it in, trying to capture and hold on to this tiny moment of pure sweet happiness.

Lorna tried to let the tenseness of her body go as they walked up the steps to the porch of the ranch house. She knew Mack had let his family know what had happened with Lyle taking Max from school and him getting hurt, so she wasn't sure what to expect when they walked through the front door.

Max had no such worries as he barreled up the stairs and let himself in.

Mack held Izzy in her car seat with one hand, and

he reached out to take her hand in his other. They felt like a team.

She wanted to feel good about that. But the thought of letting herself count on someone else terrified her. She was just starting to feel like she could count on herself. It was too hard to think about letting go of some of that control and let someone else into her life. No matter how great a kisser he was.

She needed to get her head back on straight and remember that all this relationship stuff was a ruse. The kissing was real, and she kept letting herself get caught up in the heat of it, but there was no way she was ready to let a man fully back into her life. Having Lyle back was a good reminder of why.

But it was hard to feel alone when she stepped through the front door and was engulfed in hugs and hellos from Maisie, Elizabeth, Duke, Dodge, Ford, and an assortment of big, furry dogs. Thank goodness it was only the dogs who wanted to lick her face.

"We were so worried about you," Maisie said, leading her to the big table that had already been set for supper. "You sure you and Max are okay?"

"I'm fine," she told them. "And Max is excited about getting to eat a bunch of popsicles."

"As many as I want, Aunt Maisie," Max shouted from the floor where he was the center of a cuddle puddle of golden retrievers. "Help me, Uncle Dodge." He shrieked with laughter. "I'm getting licked to death."

Mack gave her a quizzical look.

"Earlier this year, when Leni and Chevy started planning the wedding, he took to calling your brother Uncle Chevy, and I'm not sure he understood that all your brothers and Maisie and Elizabeth weren't also his aunts and uncles," she explained, then smiled at the way Dodge was on the floor ruffling both dog's bellies and her son's hair. "They all seem to like it though."

In their current situation, she was kind of glad Mack hadn't been around when that had started, since it would sound quite awkward for her son to now be calling her pretend boyfriend, "Uncle Mack'.

A knock sounded then the front door opened. One of the local deputies, Knox Garrison, stepped inside and waved to the group as he took his cowboy hat off and hung it from a peg inside the wall. "Hey, everybody."

"Hey, Knox," Dodge said, stepping forward to shake the tall cowboy's hand. "Come on in. What brings you out this way?"

"You mean besides the offer of a brisket sandwich?" Knox answered with a grin.

Lorna gaped at Mack. "I thought we weren't going to call the police."

"Mack didn't have anything to do with this," Duke said, stepping up beside her. "I told Knox I had a bunch of smoked meat left over from the wedding and that if he stopped around, I'd send him back out with a hot brisket sandwich." He touched Lorna's elbow and lowered his voice. "It's up to you if you want to talk to him about what happened this afternoon. But you know he's a good man and someone you can trust."

Ford gestured to Mack. "Knox, I don't know if you've met our little brother, Mack, yet."

"Haven't had the pleasure," the deputy said,

extending his hand to Mack. "Good to meet you. I went to high school with most of the people in this room and played hockey with a couple of your brothers."

"Good to meet you, too," Mack said, shaking Knox's hand. "But what the heck? Why does it feel like everyone I've met in this town either knows each other or somehow went to high school together?"

"Right?" Elizabeth, the only other person in the room who hadn't lived most of their lives in Woodland Hills or the neighboring town of Creedence, said. "How big was this high school?"

Dodge laughed. "Not big at all. That's why we know everyone around our age in this county. When there's only eighty-nine kids in your class, you tend to get to know them, their siblings, and all their out-of-town cousins, pretty well."

Knox shook his head. "Don't even bring up my cousin Lisa. She still talks about sneaking off to the lake with Chevy that summer she turned sixteen and visited us for the weekend." He grinned at Elizabeth. "Chevy took her midnight fishing, the boat flipped, and they both ended up in the lake."

"From what I've heard about Chevy's teenage years, it sounds more like a ploy on his part to get your cousin's clothes off," Elizabeth murmured.

As the laughter over old memories died down, Knox finally turned to her. "Hey, Lorna. Good to see you."

"Hey, Knox. You, too."

"I heard there was a little trouble with Lyle this afternoon."

"This town has too many gossips."

Knox crossed the room and lowered his voice as he spoke just to her. "Can I ask you—do you have sole custody of the kids?"

She nodded. "Yes. Lyle was so cheap, and I assume so anxious to move on with his young new girlfriend, he sent me the simplest divorce documents, which included full custody." And knowing Lyle, he probably thought giving her custody meant he wouldn't have to pay child support for a couple of kids he wasn't interested in anyway.

"Then you can file charges against him for taking Max from school grounds without your permission."

"I'm not sure…"

He shrugged. "I can just be here as an old friend, and we can leave it at that. Or I can be here in an official capacity, if you want to talk to me about what's going on. I can tell you that the more reports we have on him now will sure help when we finally get a chance to haul this guy in. And if I know Lyle Williams, we're *going* to get him for something. But it's up to you…"

He let the question hang in the air.

Funny how suddenly everyone else in the room found something to keep themselves occupied so it seemed like they weren't paying attention to their conversation at all.

Lorna wrapped her arms around her stomach. She'd spent so many years keeping this secret to herself, and Lyle had her terrified of ever involving the police in *their* family matters. Telling Knox about Lyle picking Max up from school didn't mean that much unless he knew the whole story and about the cycle of abuse.

She'd spent so much time hiding from this. But

she'd told Mack, and the sky hadn't fallen. Although, talking to Mack wasn't the same thing as filing an official police report and telling a sheriff's deputy about the abuse.

Lyle would be furious if he found out. And who knows what he would do in retaliation.

Damn it. She was so tired of walking on eggshells and doing everything to avoid making Lyle Williams mad. She was done trying to manage her *ex*-husband's temper.

She looked at Mack. He hadn't spoken up with advice or told her what to do. He'd just offered his steadfast support. And also threatened to kill Lyle—but let's stay focused on the positive. Or maybe that was the positive.

Knox stood patiently waiting for her answer.

Duke was right. Knox was a good man. She'd known him for years, and he was engaged to her hairdresser, Carley Chapman, who only ever spoke with the highest praise of all the good work he did for the community of Creedence.

She pulled in a deep breath. "Okay. Yes, let's talk."

Duke offered her a nod of encouragement then gestured toward the hallway. "You can use the office. No one will bother you."

Chapter Nineteen

TALKING TO KNOX had been easier than Lorna had thought it would be. He was a good listener, asking occasional questions as he took notes, but he mainly just let her speak. It felt a little easier after having just admitted it all to Mack. After she was done, he left her with a card and a promise to be in touch.

Duke sent him off with two smoked brisket sandwiches, and she felt lighter after he was gone. Not just like a weight had been lifted, but like it had been washed away. Like that feeling of a hot shower after three days of camping—fresh and cleansed of all the dirt and grime that had been collecting but was now scrubbed off with soap and shampoo and rinsed down the drain.

The whole atmosphere of the room had changed as the family sat down to eat, passing plates and swapping good-natured jabs and stories of the day.

Duke had baked russet potatoes and simmered green beans with slabs of bacon to go with the thick brisket sandwiches then ladled au jus into individual ramekins for each plate and offered caramelized onions and a homemade horseradish dip as condiments. The table held sour cream, shredded cheddar cheese, crumbled bacon, and more shredded brisket as toppings for the baked potatoes, and a small tray of celery, carrots, and radishes.

Talk turned to the work Ford and Elizabeth were doing on their farmhouse, and the latest issues they were having with putting in a new woodburning stove.

"You'll figure it out. You always do," Duke said, then turned to Lorna. "With these boys, when there's a problem, Dodge reads a book or studies up on how to do it, Ford is the one who digs in and builds it, and Chevy usually turns it into a party, inviting a bunch of people over to help complete the task."

"So, now I guess you have to figure out how Mack fits into that project," she said, then wished she'd kept her big mouth shut as Mack stared down at his plate.

His expression was pensive when he looked up. "I do like to read, but I'm not a scholar like Dodge, and I'm not as skilled with tools and construction as Ford, and I've never started a party in my life. I guess I'm like one of the guys who Chevy calls in to help, because I'm always willing to show up and lend a hand."

"Good to know," Ford said. "I can't promise a party, but I'll be calling you when it's time to install this stove."

"I'll be glad to help," Mack answered, and Lorna caught the small, pleased smile he wore as he reached for another helping of brisket.

"Why do have a baby monitor by your plate?" Max asked Dodge before popping a green bean into his mouth. He pointed to his little sister, who was propped up in a highchair between Lorna and Mack. "We can see the baby right there."

Dodge chuckled. "That isn't a baby monitor. It's more like a 'moo' monitor. I've got several mama cows ready to give birth, so I'm keeping an eye on them in the barn by watching them on this camera." He pointed to his phone sitting next to his plate. "I've also got an app that tells me when they're going into labor."

"How does it do that?" Lorna asked.

"It's pretty cool. It's a non-invasive sensor that attaches to the mama cow's tail, and it measures her tail's movement patterns which are triggered by the labor contractions. It collects a bunch of data, then when the cow reaches a certain level of intensity, it sends me a text. Then it's usually within an hour or so that she gives birth."

Ford chuckled. "He's even got his text programmed to sound like a loud moo when it comes in."

"It sure saves us from having to spend all night sleeping in the barn," Mack added. "Not that I wouldn't do it. I love those dang cows."

"We've got one that seems real close," Dodge said. "Her name's Junebug, and I imagine it'll be sometime tonight."

"Cool," Max said, eyeing the camera. "Can I come out to the barn with you when Junebug's gonna have her baby?"

Dodge shrugged as he looked over at Lorna. "It's okay with me, bud, but it might be in the middle of the night, so it's up to your mom."

"Pleasssse, Mommy," Max begged. "Can I go?"

"Far be it from me to stop my small child from witnessing the miracle of childbirth...or in this case, calfbirth," Lorna said. "But only if it's before midnight. Otherwise, you can just go see the new baby in the morning."

Max frowned then pointed his fork at Dodge. "You think you can ask her to try to have that baby before midnight?"

Dodge laughed. "For you, I'll sure give it a try."

"It's nice that you have a camera set up in the barn so you can keep an eye on things," Lorna said.

"Oh yeah, we've got cameras all over this place," Dodge said. "The ones in the barn are on a subscription, like the ones for your doorbell, but we've also got motion-sensor wildlife cameras set up in the pastures and the mountains around the ranch that we can check for signs of mountain lions or bears. They're mainly triggered by deer and wild turkeys, but we've caught plenty of bears and coyotes, and once even caught these two foxes playing together on it. They're more old school where you have to check the SD card, but they're free, and Gramps likes to switch the cards out then upload the photos to his laptop."

"I'd like to see a bear," Max told them.

"On the camera, please," Lorna said, ruffling her son's hair.

Max shrugged. "I'm okay either way. Mack told me if you see a bear, you're good as long as you can run faster than the guy next to you. And I'm a pretty fast runner."

The table erupted in laughter as Ford offered a solemn nod. "It's a fair point."

After supper, Ford, Dodge, and Mack shooed the women and their grandfather into the living room while they cleared the table and filled the dishwasher, then Duke served up slices of his famous Peanut Butter Pie.

"This is amazing," Lorna told Duke as she took another bite. The lusciously light peanut butter filling paired perfectly with the crunchy Oreo cookie crust. "I think I gained ten pounds just being here for supper tonight."

"Yeah, but it was worth it," Elizabeth said as she cradled a sleepy Izzy on her shoulder.

Since his brother had moved in with Elizabeth, Ford's room was free, so Lorna and the kids were sleeping in there. Mack had set up the travel crib and put a sleeping bag on one of their camping cots for Max. He and Lorna put both kids down for the night, promising to wake Max if the cow went into labor before midnight.

"Can I play a game on your phone before I go to sleep, Mommy?" Max asked as they were leaving the room.

Lorna debated the idea. "Okay, but only for ten minutes, then you have to turn it off and go to sleep."

Max frowned. "How about *twenty* minutes? Since this is like a special occasion."

"How do you figure?"

"We're having a sleepover at the ranch, so that makes it seem special."

Lorna had to concede his point. Tonight did feel special. "Okay. *Fifteen* minutes. But you have to set the timer and as soon as it goes off, you shut down the game and go to sleep." She passed the phone to her son. "I'm going to have Mack set a fifteen-minute timer, too. So, if I come back to check on you, that phone needs to be off."

The boy was already clicking through her passcode and opening the timer app. "I promise I'll turn it off right after the timer beeps."

"Okay. Good night." She leaned down and pressed a kiss to her son's blond head. He smelled like minty toothpaste, laundry detergent, and little boy, and she was tempted to pick him up and cuddle him to her. But he was already engrossed in the game.

"That kid is really smart," Mack told her as Lorna carefully pulled the bedroom door shut behind them so as not to wake Izzy.

"Yeah, he is. And he knows how to do more things on that phone than I do. Last week he Face Timed his grandma in Florida just because he missed her. I'm not sure I even know *how* to do that. But I downloaded a couple of games that are specifically to help with his dyslexia, so I don't mind having him do those before he goes to bed. They're puzzles and activities that help teach him phonics and reading and spelling. But he doesn't know that. He just thinks they're fun."

"So, not only is *he* smart, but his mom is, too."

She grinned and offered him a little extra wiggle of her hips as he followed her back into the living room.

After another round of beers and several hands of cards, Ford and Elizabeth left and Duke headed to bed. Dodge and Maisie were spending the night at the ranch, and they went to Dodge's room to watch whatever Netflix show they were binging while they waited for notifications from the moo monitors.

"You have everything you need?" Mack asked as Lorna came out of the bathroom after brushing her teeth and washing her face in preparation for bed. He'd turned out the lights in the living room but left the one above the sink in the kitchen on, and it gave off a soft glow in the otherwise darkened house.

"Yeah, I'm set," she told him. "Honestly, I'm so tired, I'm sure I'll fall asleep the second my head hits the pillow."

"Yeah, me too." He stopped outside the door to Ford's room then jerked his thumb at the next door down. "I'm right here if you need me. Or need anything, I mean." He leaned down and brushed a tender kiss against her cheek. "I'm glad you're here."

His lips were soft against her skin, and she wanted to fling her arms around his waist and bury her face in his chest. She had a sudden image of him picking her up and carrying her into his bedroom then stripping her naked and having his way with her.

Which would be super with her kids across the hall and half the Lassiter family in the surrounding rooms.

Why was she letting this man get to her?

Because he was hot as hell and had abs that made her want to lick them like hard muscled ice cream cones.

Yeah, she needed to get out of this hallway before she lost all her willpower and jumped him. "I'll see you in the morning," she said as she eased open the door so as not to wake the kids.

"Yep, sounds good. Unless you need me. Then I'm just right down the hall."

"Got it."

She'd told him that she was tired, but sleep eluded her as she lay in bed, staring at the ceiling. All she could think about was him.

Mack beat his fist into the side of his pillow, trying to mush it into a new shape. As if that might help him finally fall asleep. He'd brushed his teeth, tried to read the latest issue of the *Farm Journal*, couldn't concentrate, and had been lying in bed with his eyes wide open for the last thirty minutes rethinking everything he'd said and done with Lorna that day.

Should he have punched Lyle in the face when he'd had the chance?

Should he have kissed her goodnight outside her door in the hallway?

She was the one who had kissed him in the truck earlier that night, but he probably shouldn't have slipped his hand under her shirt.

Was there any chance she'd consider going out with him on a real date? *One that didn't have anything to do with her asshole ex-husband.*

She'd already told him she just wanted to be friends.

Why would she want a guy like me anyway? Someone his own mother didn't even want.

He rolled over on his back and stared at the ceiling.

What if she was still awake? Maybe he should text her. Make sure she's okay.

No, the phone could wake up the kids.

His mind strayed to the little pair of pajama shorts she'd been wearing and how they'd barely covered her luscious ass. And not that he'd been looking, but he was pretty sure she wasn't wearing a bra under the matching pajama top.

He turned his head as he thought he heard a sound in the hallway. It could have been his brother or Duke. Or nothing.

It wouldn't hurt to just look out the door though. Maybe it was Lorna, going to the kitchen for a drink of water. Maybe he could catch her there and have another chance at a better good night kiss.

He climbed out of bed, pulled on a pair of loose gray sweats, and padded barefoot to the door. The noise had probably just been the house settling.

Pulling open the door, his mouth went dry at the sight of Lorna standing there, her fist raised as if she were about to knock.

"Oh, hi," she said, dropping her hand and wrapping her arms around her body as she shifted from one foot to the other. "I was just…"

"Yeah, me too," he said, staring at her as if he couldn't quite believe she was there. Like she might be a mirage, or maybe he really had fallen asleep, and this was just a dream.

Either way, he wasn't missing out on another opportunity. He took a step back and opened the door wider. She didn't say anything as she slipped through, and he shut the door behind her.

She turned and looked up at him. The room was lit only by the silvery glow of moonlight shining through the window. She lifted a hand and pressed it to his chest, and he shivered at the touch of her fingers on his bare skin.

Her voice was soft, but there was no mistaking her words as she stared into his eyes. "Take me."

He swallowed, then leaned in and crushed her mouth with his. Her arms wrapped around his neck, her fingers tunneling through his hair then grasping fists of it as he deepened the kiss, his tongue exploring her mouth as one of his hands slid under her shirt and palmed her breast while the other reached down to cup her perfect ass.

There were too many clothes between them. He needed to see her, to touch her, to have her skin against his.

Lifting her up, he carried her to his bed and laid her on the mattress. But she sat up, reached for the waistband of his sweats, and pulled them and his boxer briefs down.

Okay, this really must be a dream.

But if it was, he sure as hell didn't want to wake up as she leaned forward and ran her tongue down the length of his shaft before drawing him into her mouth.

He let out a groan as her lips skimmed back and forth, tugging and sucking, eradicating his control as he lost himself in the sensations.

Just when his small amount of control was slipping, she drew back and pulled him down on the bed with her.

She'd had her turn.

Now he wanted his.

Rocking back on his knees, he hooked his fingers under the elastic of both her pajama bottoms and her panties and wrenched them down her legs. Her top had shifted up just enough for him to glimpse the creamy flesh of one breast, and he filled his hand with it as he used his other to spread her legs.

Dipping his head, he planted a kiss on the tender inner spot on her thigh that had driven her nuts the night before.

He couldn't believe that he was getting to have this woman again, but he wasn't questioning it. He was too absorbed in the essence of her, the way she smelled, the softness of her skin, the muted moans she made when he grazed her thigh with the whiskers on his jaw.

He tried to take it slow, to tease and tempt, but he had to taste her.

Only, she sat up and pushed him back instead, kissing his neck and nipping at his chest before climbing on top of him. He reached for the bedside drawer, grabbed a foil packet and covered himself before she straddled him, her hips already grinding against his as she reached for the hem of her shirt, then pulled it over her head and tossed it to the floor.

"My god, you're gorgeous," he whispered, his voice husky with desire, as he stared in wonder at her beautiful body. Reaching up, he filled his hands with her breasts and elicited one of her soft kitten sighs as he rolled her taut nipples between his fingers.

Rock hard, he rubbed against her center as she writhed over him, arching her back and offering him an even better view.

She reached between them and guided him into her. Letting out a growl, he gripped her thighs, digging his fingers into her flesh as she rode him. Her hair was loose and wild, and she had a reckless abandon about her as she took what she wanted from him.

The night before she had submitted to him, but

tonight it felt like she needed to be the one in control. And he was only too happy to let her be, almost losing his own control as he watched her run her hands over her belly and touch herself, taking charge of her own pleasure.

He recognized this for the gift it was—Lorna offering herself to him—so freely, still in control, but without inhibitions or reserve.

He'd spent the months in Texas fantasizing about her, dreaming of being with her, kissing her, touching her, but this was beyond anything he'd imagined. Everything about her felt so damn good.

Her breasts were lush perfection, and as she leaned forward, he pressed up to suck the tip of one taut nipple into his mouth. She squirmed over him, around him, and his control teetered on the edge.

Her movements quickened, and he could tell by the expression on her face and the way her fingers dug into his hip that she was close to the edge herself.

Arching his hips, he gave her everything she wanted, lost in the sweet ecstasy of her pleasure. Then her hands flattened on his chest, and she pressed her lips together as if in an effort not to cry out as she soared over the edge. And took her with him.

They knew they weren't alone in the house, and trying to give and take pleasure while keeping quiet suddenly became a fun way to tease and tantalize each other.

She was driving him crazy, but they were having fun, and he was falling harder and harder for this woman.

He loved the way she laughed, the way her hair fell over her shoulders, the way she smiled coyly at him as she drew him to the brink of desire. Being with her was a gift he'd never imagined getting.

He pressed his lips together, stifling another groan as she straddled him again, but this time giving him a different view.

Then a knock sounded on his door and Dodge called out, "I just got the moo text. Junebug's been in labor for thirty minutes. Meet us in the barn if you want to meet her calf."

Chapter Twenty

"OH SHIT," LORNA said, then covered the giggle trying to escape her mouth as she and Mack scrambled from the bed and tried to find their clothes. Thank goodness Dodge had only knocked and not opened the door to tell his brother about the cow in labor.

She'd never be able to look him in the eye if he'd caught her naked and riding his brother in Reverse Cowgirl.

Mack tossed her panties toward her then shimmied into his boxer briefs and the pair of jeans he'd left on the chair beside the bed. She pulled her pajamas back on as quickly as she could then tried not to drool as he tugged a black T-shirt over his broad, muscled chest. A chest she had just been kissing and running her hands over.

A folded stack of Mack's flannel shirts sat on the dresser, and she grabbed the top one and pulled it on over her pajamas. Probably shouldn't show up to the barn and let everyone know she didn't have a bra on.

"I need to grab some shoes," she told Mack as he was pulling on his boots.

She opened the door to see her son come flying out of their bedroom, his hair poking up in all directions and his cowboy boots pulled on over his Paw Patrol pajamas. His eyes were wild as he looked up at her. "I heard Dodge say he got the moo-call. And the clock by the bed says eleven two zero, so it's before twelve." He didn't seem to mind that his boots were on the wrong feet as he ran down the hall, waving her along with him. "Come on Mommy, we don't want to miss Junebug having her calf."

"All right, let me put my shoes on." *And maybe a bra too.*

"I'll take him out," Mack said, brushing back his shock of dark hair and pulling a ball cap on backwards over it as he came through the door behind her. "You can come out when you're ready." He scooped Max up in his arms as he headed for the front door. "Yee haw, buddy. Let's go meet a new baby calf."

By the time Lorna pulled on some sweatpants, her sneakers, and a bra, and made it out to the barn, the blessed event was in full swing. And she seemed to be the last one to the party.

One section of the barn had been set up with pens to hold the pregnant cows, and the group were all around one pen that held a red and white cow who Lorna assumed was Junebug.

Duke had a firm hand on Max's shoulder, probably to keep him from climbing into the pen with the cow, as they kept an eye on the action through the bars of the makeshift corral.

Maisie looked adorable with her glasses on, and her mess of curly hair pulled into a bun on top of her head. She wore ankle-high pink Ropers and what

Lorna assumed was one of Dodge's Carhartt hoodies over a mid-calf nightgown that had little blue flowers on it, which looked both boho-chic and also like something out of her grandma's closet—but Maisie pulled it off.

Dodge and Mack were in the pen with the cow, both leaning over her and offering words of encouragement as they ran their hands over her belly.

"How's it going?" she asked Duke.

He shook his head, a concerned expression on his face. "Not great. The calf is in breach, and the boys are trying to turn it."

Lorna pressed her hands to her stomach, trying not to imagine the pain the cow must be feeling as the two strong cowboys tried to shift the calf around inside her belly. "Can they do that?"

"Let's hope so," he said. "Otherwise, we might lose her and the calf."

"How could you lose her?" Max asked. "She's right in front of us."

Lorna smiled down at her sweet son, thankful he didn't understand Duke's true meaning. She sent up a silent prayer for the life of both mother and baby.

Mack pushed his sleeve up, doused his arm with the soapy water in a bucket by the gate then went in shoulder deep to try to retrieve the calf. "I've got her back legs," he told Dodge. "Can you try to push her rump forward?"

The two of them worked together, straining and adjusting until Mack finally pulled his arm out with two small hooves clutched in his hand.

"I need the chains," he said.

Duke passed him a set of chains with steel handles

attached to them, and he hooked the chains around the hooves then leaned back, holding a handle in each hand as he braced his boots against the bars of the pen.

"Come on, baby girl," Mack cooed to the cow. "I know this hurts, but I need your help. We'll take it slow." He pulled gently as the cow let out a painful bawl. "I know, baby. I'm here."

The hooves slowly came forward as Mack pulled and Dodge inserted lubricant and massaged the cow's belly, both trying to move the calf through the birth canal.

Duke's whole body seemed tense as he leaned closer to speak quietly to Lorna. "Once they get to a certain spot, they've got to get it out quickly, otherwise it could suffocate because its head is still inside the cow when the umbilical cord pinches off or breaks. This kind of thing is always dangerous to the survival of the calf and the health of the mama cow."

"Mack seems like he's done this before," she said, amazed at the skill both he and Dodge were showing as they worked together to ease more of the calf out.

Duke nodded. "He's been involved in ranching his whole adult life. And he's damn good at it. We're lucky to have him."

Mack's muscles strained as he leaned back and pulled with the cow's next contraction. "We got this, baby," he said, releasing the hooks of the handles and moving them up the chains to get better traction.

"Do you want me to grab the calf jack?" Dodge asked.

"Nah, I think we can do it," Mack told him. "The hips are almost through."

"What's a calf jack?" Lorna asked Duke.

He pointed to a steel contraption leaning against the wall. It had a large U-shaped piece on one end of a steel handle with a ratchet mechanism connected to a steel cable. "It's used to help pull the calf out if the guys can't do it. They'll hook that cable to the hooves then position the U-shaped part around her backside, then ratchet the cable tighter until it pulls the calf free."

Lorna winced, the memories of giving birth to Izzy still fresh in her mind.

"That's it, sweet girl," Mack told the cow as he gritted his teeth and gave another pull. "You can do it."

The cow's stomach gave another heave, then the hips were through, and the baby calf slid into the straw.

"It's out," Mack said, dropping the handles and quickly working to strip the remains of the amniotic sac from its legs and hind quarters. "And of course, it's a boy. It's always the boys who give us trouble." Sticking his fingers into the calf's mouth, he tried to clear any mucous, but it didn't seem to be breathing.

Lorna pulled Max closer to her legs, terrified that her son had just witnessed a dead calf being pulled and praying that Mack could save his life.

He grabbed a piece of straw and circled it around inside the calf's nostrils.

"He's tickling inside its nose to try to get it to sneeze or start breathing," Maisie explained, squeezing her hand as they watched Duke kneel down and start rubbing the calf vigorously with a towel. "He's trying to stimulate his breathing and circulation. The towel is supposed to mimic the natural licking of the calf that the mother would be doing. She just looks too worn out to do it yet. But it can also help a weak calf to regulate its body temperature and start breathing on its own."

"Is he gonna be okay, Mama?" Max asked, his voice small and frightened.

The calf let out a sneeze and a wheeze, and everyone in the barn seemed to let out a sigh of relief accompanied by a whoop from Mack.

They dragged the calf closer to the mama cow's head, and she licked at his head and body to clean him. He was all red except for a small white tuft in the middle of his forehead, a bit of white on his belly and white socks on both his back legs and one of his fronts.

"Yes," Mack said, grinning over at her son. "He is going to be okay."

They all cheered then as Mack pushed to his feet and used another towel to clean off his arms and chest. He knelt beside Max and pointed at the baby cow. "That calf is yours."

Max frowned. "What do you mean?"

Lorna was thinking the same thing. This was news to her, and she wasn't sure she was prepared for the care and feeding of a small cow.

"I mean, I talked to my brothers and Duke, and we want you to have Junebug's calf," Mack told him.

Her son's face lit with delight. "Can I bring him home and he can sleep in my bedroom?"

Mack chuckled. "No, he has to stay here where his mama can take care of him."

Whew. Thank goodness for that.

"But you can pick his name, and you can visit him whenever you want," Mack continued. "And if you spend a lot of time with him when he's little like this, and give him lots of love and occasional treats, he'll recognize you and come to you when you come out to see him."

Max beamed up at his mother then threw his arms around Mack's neck, oblivious to the muck and straw on his chest. Thank goodness she'd brought extra pajamas. "My very own cow. I can't believe it. I will love him and bring him treats. This is the best night ever." He pulled back as his small brow furrowed. "What kind of treats does a cow like anyway?"

Chapter Twenty-One

MACK REPORTED FOR barista duty the next morning promptly at seven. Lorna had left the ranch twenty minutes before him so she could drop the kids off with Gertie. Max had an odd schedule because it was the last day of school, so Gertie was going to take him in then he and Lorna would pick him up from school that afternoon.

They'd invited him to go to the school carnival with them that night, and he was oddly looking forward to it. Not the part about hanging around with a bunch of elementary school kids and their parents and playing silly carnival games, but the part about where he got to do all that with Lorna, Max, and Izzy.

They were starting to feel like family to him, and that both excited and scared the hell out of him. When he'd first arrived in Woodland Hills the summer before, they had all hung out together quite a bit, he and his brothers and their girlfriends, and Lorna and the kids, and he'd had the same kind of feelings then—like he was actually part of something. Part of a family.

He'd been scared then, too. And looking back now, he had to wonder if maybe that was a portion of the reason he'd agreed to go back to Texas. And maybe why he'd stayed away.

He'd yearned for a family for so long, but then when he finally got one, it was a bit overwhelming and terrifying. In his life, whenever anything started to go well for him, like having Anna Maria and her family take him in and treat him like one of theirs, it got taken away.

Or whenever he thought things might be going okay with his mom, she'd end up taking off again and making him feel like a chump for believing for once, things might be different.

But this time, with Lorna and the kids, it did feel different. It felt real. Which was kind of a joke, since they were supposed to be in a *fake* relationship.

He knew that. But still, a part of him wanted it to be real—wanted this to be his life. The American dream—a beautiful woman and two point five kids. Although, in their case, they'd have to count their point five as the new baby cow.

"Hey, Mack," Lorna called, breaking into his thoughts as she waved him toward the back door. "Would you take a look at something with me real quick?"

"Sure." He followed her outside then frowned as she pointed to the back door where it looked like someone had taken a screwdriver to the lock. "What the hell?"

"Is it just me, or does this look like somebody might have tried to break into my shop last night?"

"That's exactly what it looks like. And I'll give you three guesses as to who that somebody might be."

"I think I only need one."

"Thank goodness he didn't get in." Mack studied the scratches around the lock. "Or do you think he did? Have you checked to make sure nothing is missing?"

"No, I haven't checked anything. I just got here a few minutes ago and wanted to bring a dish of dog food out here for Mocha…uh…I mean, the stray dog." She offered him a sheepish grin then it disappeared as she turned back to the door. "I saw this as I was coming back inside."

They checked on the dog, who was inside her crate and had already wolfed down the dog food Lorna had given her, then went in and checked the back office, the safe, and the dining area, but nothing seemed amiss.

"He must not have been able to break in," Lorna said.

"I think we should call the police anyway. Do you still have Knox's card?"

She nodded. "It's in my purse."

Lorna locked up the coffee shop at exactly two that afternoon. It had been a busy day, probably made busier by everyone coming in and wanting to know why a deputy sheriff's truck was parked in the alley behind the shop.

Thank goodness for Mack. He might not know the difference between a *capp*uccino and a *frapp*uccino, but he was great with people. He was attentive and funny and had the customers who were waiting in line laughing and joking around so much that no one complained that she was the only one fixing drinks or that it took her a bit longer to get their orders up.

For his part, Mack was a quick study and over the past few days had learned to make a few of the simpler drinks. He could pour black coffees, make espressos, froth milk, and do all the teas, plus heat up and plate the baked goods.

Selling over a hundred coffees that day was great for business, but hell on her back and feet, and all she wanted to do was go home and stand under a hot shower for an hour. But the school was having their end of year carnival that night, and she and Max were signed up to run a booth for an hour.

She might be able to close the coffee shop for the afternoon, but the duties of a mother never ended. And Max was so excited about the school carnival. He'd been talking about it for weeks.

Plus, it was hilarious that she even dreamed of standing in the shower for an hour. With her life, she was lucky to get five minutes. Although, since a certain hot cowboy had come back into her life, she had been taking a few extra minutes to keep her legs shaved.

"You ready?" Mack asked, untying the apron from his waist then folding it neatly and placing it on the edge of the counter to be ready for his shift in the morning. Funny how his was still clean while hers had gone in the hamper in her office because it was covered in coffee grounds and splashed syrups, whipped cream, and espresso.

It had been fun working with Mack that week. Maybe too fun.

She was starting to count on seeing him every day and looked forward to his texts and calls when they weren't together. And not just seeing him but touching him as well. Their fake-dating ruse required them to occasionally hold hands or for Mack to put his arm around her or brush her cheek with a kiss, and she would be lying if she said she wasn't enjoying that part of the scheme.

She prayed that Lyle would leave town and leave her alone, sooner rather than later, but then what reason would Mack have for pretending to be her boyfriend?

"Yes, just let me grab my purse," she told him. "Check the fridge. I made us a couple of iced coffees to go."

The weather was perfect for a walk, and they sipped their coffees and held hands while they meandered down to the grade school with the Colorado sunshine warming their faces.

They made it to the school a few minutes before the bell rang, so they sat on a bench outside and chatted easily about their day and their plans for that night. Mack offered to watch Izzy for the hour that she and Max ran the Ring Toss booth, and even though she readily agreed, she wondered if she shouldn't start pulling back and quit counting on him for so much.

Her son's face lit with excitement when he saw Mack waiting with her, and he hugged them both then talked nonstop the whole way back to the coffee shop where she'd left the minivan.

Mack was going back to the ranch for a few hours

to catch up on chores but planned to pick them up around five so they could all go to the school together.

"Oh, shoot, I forgot to get cash for tonight," she told Mack as they were loading the kids into the van. "Can you finish buckling and keep an eye on these two for a second while I run in real quick and raid the petty cash box?"

"Sure," Mack told her, clicking Izzy into her seat.

She kept a metal box with a few hundred dollars in assorted small bills in the bottom drawer of her desk, just in case she needed it for deliveries or tips or if one of the employees had to run to the grocery store to grab an extra gallon of milk. Or, apparently, if she needed a couple of spare twenties for the school carnival.

Plopping down into the desk chair, she pulled out the small metal box, and terror seized her heart as she lifted the lid.

CHAPTER TWENTY-TWO

LORNA STARED INTO the box. It was empty, except for the bottom half of a piece of pink paper which had been torn from the notepad on her desk.

Her hands trembled as she picked up the note and recognized Lyle's handwriting.

A sob caught in her throat as she read the words. *"Whatever you have belongs to me too."*

So, he *had* broken in.

What else had he done while he was inside her office? Her shop? Her space that she had so lovingly created on her own.

And that now was sullied by his very presence.

It appeared that all he had done was steal the money from the petty cash box. Oh, and left a terrifying note behind to let her know that he could get to her. No matter how many locked doors she put between them, no matter how many tall cowboys were in her life, he would *always* be able to get to her.

She stuffed the note in her pocket and slammed the box shut, her eyes madly searching the room to spot any other signs he had been there. Nothing else seemed amiss.

Forgetting about the money for the carnival, she hurried back outside, taking a few extra seconds to double-check that she'd locked the front door behind her. Although now she had to wonder if it even mattered.

She took a deep breath and tried to calm her racing heart as she walked toward the minivan where Mack was standing with the side door open and deep in apparent conversation with her son about why frogs were green.

He looked up at her, and his happy expression clouded. "What's wrong?"

"Nothing." She'd tried to keep her voice steady, but it had come out hoarse.

"You're white as a sheet. What happened?"

She cleared her throat and tried again for a calm nonchalance. It wouldn't help anything for her kids to see her upset. "It's nothing, really. But it seems like our friend *did* get into the shop after all. The petty cash box was empty."

She would tell him about the threatening note later. Now was not the time. Not in front of the kids.

She turned away and lowered her voice so her son wouldn't hear. "We can talk about it later."

"*And* give Knox a call," Mack said.

"Yes, but after the carnival. Max is so excited about tonight. I don't want anything to take that away from him."

He nodded. "Okay. I can respect that. What do you need from me?"

"Nothing. I'm good."

His face fell. Then he pulled her to him. "Well, I'm giving you a hug anyway."

She'd take it. In fact, she wanted to melt into him and have him take all this craziness and drama away. But she knew she couldn't put that on him.

She had to figure this out on her own.

She had to decide how to stand up to this bully who had terrorized her for so many years. She had to do it for herself. But mainly for her children.

And to do any of that, she needed time to think. By herself.

She drew in a deep breath as she pulled away. "Thank you. I'd better get these kids home. We'll see you in a few hours."

"I'll be there," he said.

"Save room for a corn dog," Max called to him as he headed for his truck. "And some funnel cake."

Mack smiled at her son and waved. "Don't worry. I've always got room for funnel cake."

The carnival was in full swing as Lorna leaned over and picked up the three rings of the final toss of her and Max's shift and passed them to the parent and child who were taking over for the next shift.

She'd tried to put Lyle's threatening note—and the fact that he'd broken into her shop—out of her mind and keep her focus on the precious time she was getting to spend with Max.

They'd had fun running the booth together, taking turns on who had to pick up the rings and who got to hand out the cheesy plastic prizes, but she was ready to sit down and have one of those funnel cakes they'd talked about earlier.

They'd arrived at the school a few hours ago and had enough time to eat corn dogs and curly fries and wander around most of the booths before she and Max had to report for ring toss duty. But her son was far from being done with hanging out at the carnival.

He still had plans to try his hand at winning a prize in the cake walk, and doing the basketball shoot, the fishing game, and the balloon pop. And he'd talked Mack into running the parent/kid three-legged race with him later. Mack wasn't his parent, but the rules were pretty lenient where the family member was concerned, and she was just thankful that it was Mack who had to make a fool of himself instead of her.

She scanned the crowd for the tall cowboy, and grinned as she saw him walking toward them, a happy Izzy strapped in the carrier on his chest. He had a large cup of lemonade in one hand and a funnel cake in the other.

"I thought you'd be ready for this," he told her, leaning down to brush her cheek with a kiss. He smelled sweet and the dusting of powdered sugar on his face suggested he might have already sampled a piece.

She tickled the toes and nuzzled the neck of Izzy, who was facing forward in the baby carrier. Mack seemed to always know what she needed. "Thank you. I am *so* ready. That ring toss business is hard work." She took a sip of the lemonade then brushed the sugar from his cheek, and tried not to think about how comfortable she was doing both acts that were so intimate in nature. It had been years since she'd so casually touched another man's face or shared a straw. "Looks like you might have already tried the funnel cake."

He grinned again. "Guilty. But I swear I didn't give any to Izzy."

She laughed. "That's a relief. Funnel cake is not usually on the approved list of solids for infants."

"But it is on the list for six-year-olds," Max said, squeezing between them. "So, pass me a piece, would ya?"

Lorna laughed again—she sure had been doing a lot of that in the last several days—as they found a place to sit at one of the lunch tables in the center of the cafeteria, which also served as the gymnasium.

"Izzy and I have been having a great time," Mack told her, palming the baby's tummy in his large hand and jiggling it to make her smile. "Haven't we, baby girl? We checked out all the booths again and took a walk outside. They've got a little petting zoo set up by the playground we missed when we were walking around earlier. *And* we won a chocolate cake and two dozen peanut butter cookies in the cake walk."

"Oh shoot. How many times did you do it?" Lorna asked.

"And where's the cake?" Max wanted to know.

Mack laughed. "It made Izzy giggle, so I think we did it five or six times, and I ate three of the cookies then put the rest of them *and* the cake in the minivan to share when we get home."

When we get home.

The words hit her like a punch to the chest, and she put her head down and took another sip of lemonade—not quite sure why the tears had just sprung to her eyes. They had come so easily out of Mack's mouth, and even now, as she stuffed another piece of funnel cake in her mouth, they were sitting in her gut like a stone she had swallowed.

This pretend relationship sure brought up a whole lot of real feelings.

Thank goodness there were funnel cakes and kettle corn to stuff them down with.

"Let's go," Max said.

"Yeah, we need to go if we're going to get through all these tickets," Mack said, pulling a stack of tickets from the pocket of the baby carrier.

"Oh no," Lorna said. "You didn't have to buy all those." She'd scrounged around her house that afternoon and had come up with a ten-dollar bill, several singles and six quarters, so she had enough to buy at least a few tickets that night.

"I know I didn't have to," Mack said. "But I wanted to. All the money goes to support the school, and I'm having fun. I love all this stuff."

She frowned, weighing her guilt for letting him treat them to all those tickets with the joy Max would get from spending them.

Mack nudged her shoulders. "I never got to go to a school carnival as a kid. And if I *had* been able to go, I never would have had the money to buy handfuls of tickets. Let me do this. Please."

She hadn't weighed Mack's happiness or the reasons behind his generosity into her decision. She did now.

"Okay, let's go blow a buttload of tickets."

Max's eyes went wide as he clapped his hand over her mouth. "You said *butt*."

She laughed then let her son drag them all over the

gymnasium, where he won four cheesy plastic toys and a small stuffed cow he said reminded him of his new calf.

"Hi, Aunt Maisie," Max called, running up to his favorite librarian, who was running a booth for the library.

She stood in front of a wide bookshelf, painted bright pink and stuffed with picture books. In front of her was a large shallow plastic tub filled with water and about twenty-five rubber ducks floating around in it.

"Hi, Max," Maisie said. "Do you want to pick a duck? If there's a picture of a book underneath it, then you get to choose one of these books as a prize."

Mack handed over five tickets.

Max picked a neon blue duck, and his face lit up as he turned it over. "There's a picture of a book."

Maisie clapped her hands with delight. "Wow. You won a prize, Max. Great job."

Mack leaned close to Lorna's ear, his warm powdered sugar-scented breath sending a pleasant shiver down her spine. "Why do I have a feeling every one of those ducks has a picture of a book underneath it?"

Lorna grinned as she gave him an affirmative nod.

Max picked a book about dinosaurs. "Can we read this one at the library next week, Aunt Maisie?"

"Sure. That's a great idea," she said. "And I have a few others already set aside that I think you're gonna love."

"We're so grateful to have Maisie in our lives," Lorna told Mack. "When she found out about Max, she took a course on how to help kids with dyslexia, and she's offered to tutor him and another little girl this summer to help them with their reading, so they don't fall behind going into school next year."

"That's really cool," he said.

"A lot of it is just spending time listening to him read. It takes a surprising amount of patience."

Mack shrugged. "If there's anything I've learned in the life of a cowboy, it's how to be patient. So, I'm happy to listen to him read anytime, too."

She didn't know what to say. "That's a kind offer," she finally managed, then turned to see Ford and Elizabeth walking up to them and waved.

Elizabeth had the same stuffed cow as Max, and he set his new book down to pull it from his pocket and hold it up to show her. "Look, Aunt 'lizabeth, we have the same one. Did you hear that Mack gave me my very own calf? I decided to name him Kevin, 'cause that's my favorite minion's name, so this one is Stuart, because that's my second favorite minion's name. And I can sleep with this one at my house. My mommy said I can't bring my real calf home because it won't fit in my bed."

"Your mommy is very smart," Elizabeth told him. "And Kevin is a great name. I'm looking forward to meeting him."

An announcement blared through the gymnasium letting everyone know there was still kettle corn left, that the parent/child three-legged race was about to start, and that if anyone was missing a black lab wearing a red collar, to please collect him at the corn dog stand.

Max made some corny joke about a dog eating a

corn dog, and Lorna was laughing until she turned around and ran into Lyle.

"Well, isn't this a nice little family outing?" he said, the disdain evident in his tone as he raked his gaze over the four of them, pausing to sneer at Mack and the baby strapped to his chest. "Does she make you carry the diaper bag, too? Or do you put her things in your man-purse?"

The fact that Lyle would compare carrying his child to a diaper bag made Lorna want to hurl. How could she have ever been married to this man?

"Hey, kid," he said to Max, but made no move to hug him or Izzy. "Whatcha got there?"

Max held up the stuffed toy. "It's a cow. But Mack just gave me a real calf. His name is Kevin, and he's all mine."

"Yeah? That's cool. When he gets big and fat, you can sell him for steaks and make a nice chunk of money."

Max looked horrified and moved closer to her. "I'm never selling him. He's gonna be my best friend."

Lyle raised a judgmental eyebrow at Lorna. "You're letting the kid have a cow? The way I remember, you wouldn't even let him have a dog in the house."

No. Lyle was the one who wouldn't let any pets in the house. He hated any kind of mess and never wanted to spend the extra money to feed an animal.

But she wasn't going to argue with him. "It's staying out on the ranch."

Mack's family and a few other people were gathered around them, not actively eavesdropping but for sure paying attention to their conversation. Two exes and the new boyfriend having a conversation would be a hot gossip topic in this town.

"We gotta go," Max said, pulling on her arm. "The three-legged race is about to start."

"I just heard the announcement for that," Lyle said, then looked down at Max. "It's for parents and kids, right? You want me to do that with you instead of your mom, kid?"

Max took a step back and pushed against Mack's leg. "No, thanks. I'm doing it with Mack."

"Mack? You mean this guy?" Lyle jerked a thumb at the cowboy. His voice held the barely concealed rage Lorna had heard so many times as he said, "But he isn't one of your parents."

"It's fine," Lorna said, trying to head off an argument.

"No, it's not fine," Lyle said, raising his voice. "That race is for kids and their *parent*, and last I checked, *I'm* this kid's dad."

Not that he'd acted like it at any point in the last few years.

"*This kid* has a name." Mack's jaw was set, and his shoulders were back as he took a step toward Lyle. "And Max asked me to do the race with him, so that's what we're going to do."

She didn't think Mack would actually start something with Lyle, especially not with Izzy strapped to his chest, but there was enough of menace in his tone, that she worried her ex would feel threatened and try something stupid.

Lyle lifted his chin, that hard glint of meanness in his eye as he sneered at Mack. "You wanna take this outside?"

Yep. That was something stupid, all right.

Dodge and Ford stepped up to either side of Mack, and Lyle shrunk back.

"I think it's time for you to go," Mack told him. "This is a family event, and I'm choosing to respect that. Why don't you do the same."

"Why don't you fuck off?" Lyle growled, but he turned and stomped away, sweeping a paper tray holding the remains of a hotdog off the end of a table and sending a red spray of ketchup flying.

Max's bottom lip was trembling, and Lorna crouched down and pulled her son into a hug. "It's okay, honey."

"I didn't mean to make him mad. Is he gonna hurt you now, Mommy?"

His words were like a knife to her heart. She'd always tried to hide as much of Lyle's violence toward her from her son, but kids were perceptive, and apparently Max knew more than she'd thought.

"No, baby. And *you* didn't *make* him mad. I think he was already mad and was just looking to pick a fight. But he's gone now." Maybe they should just leave too. But then that would be letting Lyle win. She pulled back and wiped her son's tears from his cheeks. "And you have a three-legged race to run. We'd better get out there. And I'll bet Uncle Ford and Uncle Dodge will even come out and cheer you and Mack on."

"We wouldn't miss it," Dodge said, chuckling as he nudged Mack.

Elizabeth had already picked up the trash Lyle had thrown and found some napkins to clean the ketchup from the floor. "We'll be right out," she called.

Mack held his hand out to her son. "Come on, bud. Let's go win this race."

As it turned out, Mack and Max did *not* win the race. A mother-daughter team with a tall kindergartener and a short mother were apparently a better matched pair, and they easily stole the blue ribbon.

But Mack and her son sure had fun, laughing their heads off as they goofily walked and tried to jog and especially when Mack stumbled, and they both almost fell. They did each get a participation ribbon though, which Mack said he would put on the refrigerator as soon as he got home.

Lorna had taken Izzy from Mack, and the baby giggled along with her as she laughed and cheered for their two guys.

It was a good way to end the carnival, and Mack bought them a bag of kettle corn for the ride home. Izzy fell asleep on the short drive, and Mack carried her car seat into the house, while she unbuckled the tired six-year-old.

It was just after nine when they finally got both kids to bed, tucking Max's new stuffed cow, Stuart, in with him, and they were coming down the stairs when a knock sounded at the door.

It was Maisie and Dodge.

The librarian held up a picture book with a dinosaur on the cover. "Max forgot his book."

"We were walking by and thought we'd drop it off," Dodge said.

Maisie offered her a gentle smile. "And make sure you were okay."

Lorna was touched by their thoughtfulness. "I'm fine." Her phone buzzed in her pocket, and she pulled it out to see Barb Johnson's name on the screen. Barb and her husband owned a pet store across the alley from the coffee shop. It was strange that Barb would be calling her, especially this late, and a sense of foreboding filled her chest as she answered the phone. "Hi Barb, everything okay?"

She reached for Mack's hand as she listened to her neighbor's words, and his expression turned concerned as she imagined the color had probably just drained from her face.

He, Dodge, and Maisie were staring at her as she said, "I'll be right there," then shoved the phone in her pocket. She knew she needed to run out the door, but she felt frozen in shock. "That was Barb Johnson. She said the coffee shop is on fire."

Chapter Twenty-Three

Mack squeezed her hand, and Lorna finally stirred into action, grabbing her purse and the car keys from the side table by the door. She turned back to Maisie. "Can you stay with the kids for me? They're both already asleep."

"Yes, of course," Maisie said. "You guys go. We'll be fine."

"I'll drive," Mack told her as he ran out the door behind her.

It only took a few minutes to get downtown, and the lights and noise of the firetruck led them to the alley behind the shop. Mack parked as close as he could, then they were both out of the truck and running, splashing through the puddles made by the hose of the fire engine.

Three firemen were spraying down the back of the building where black char marks now soiled the red brick.

The fire appeared to be out, but there was a lot of smoke and some damage to the back of the building. A pile of ash and rubble was where the stack of wooden pallets had previously been.

"Oh no," Lorna cried, then shouted, "Mocha! Here, girl." Tears were already streaming down her cheeks. She couldn't breathe. Not just because of the thick smoke in the air, but from the terror that the little dog had perished in the fire. "Mocha!" she screamed again, trying to get closer to the building.

Please God. Please God.

Smoke burned her eyes. She blinked against it as she scanned the alley.

A dumpster sat between her shop and the next one over, and she swore she heard a small bark coming from that direction.

"Mack! She's there!" She pointed to the spot as she sprinted behind the firemen and dropped to her knees, trying to peer into the blackness behind the dumpster. She gagged at the scent of garbage and charred wood.

Mack was standing above her and shone the flashlight from his phone into the dark area.

Far back, against a filthy cardboard box, cowered the little dog, now almost all black with the soot covering her fur.

"Come here, baby," Lorna cooed, holding her arms out and praying just this once, that the dog would come to her.

It let out a whimper and inched forward then paused as it stared at Lorna, as if trying to make a decision. Then it barked again and ran toward her, leaping into her lap. The dog was shaking as she cuddled it to her chest. "It's okay. I've got you. You're okay," she told the sweet pup as it burrowed against her.

Mack helped her up and hugged both her and the dog to him. "I've got you both," he said into her hair as he pulled them tighter against him. The dog squirmed then licked her chin as one of the volunteer firemen, a guy who frequently came into the coffee shop and ordered a caramel latte with a triple shot of espresso approached them.

"We've got the fire out. Good news is that it was contained to the outside of the building. Did you have a bunch of wood piled up back here?"

Lorna nodded. "A big stack of wooden pallets. I was saving them to eventually take home and use to try to make a porch swing." She didn't know why she told him that detail. It didn't matter. But her brain wasn't quite processing things like it should.

I'm probably in shock.

"Well, sorry, but you're going to have to save some new ones. Did you store anything else back here around those pallets?"

She shook her head. "No. I guess I had a little crate with a blanket and a couple of dishes for the dog, but that's it. Why?"

"There was a pretty strong smell of gasoline, and the burn marks indicate the fire started around that wood." He lowered his voice. "There appears to be some pour patterns on the patio too, suggesting this might have been intentionally set. Maybe some kids were screwing around back here. We'll write up a report, and let you know what we find."

Some kids? Doubtful. This had Lyle Williams' name written all over it.

But she wasn't sure if she should mention his name. If this was his retaliation for a slight rift at the school carnival, what would he do if she accused him of arson?

It took another hour before the fire truck left and all the bystanders drifted away. Ford and Elizabeth had shown up to offer support, but there wasn't much for any of them to do. She'd checked inside the building, taking the dog in to get her some water, but everything seemed fine inside the coffee shop.

It wasn't until much later that night, after they'd gone back to her house and given the dog a good bath and some fresh food and water, after Dodge and Maisie had gone home, and she and Mack had both showered and washed the scent of smoke from their skin and hair, that Lorna finally had the chance to tell him about the note she'd found earlier that day.

"It was in the petty cash box. The money was gone, and this was left inside." She handed him the folded piece of paper.

He frowned down at the message. "Who the hell does this guy think he is?"

She let out a sigh but could only shrug in answer.

"Okay, this is pure bullshit," Mack said, handing her the note back. "But it doesn't help make sense of what happened tonight. If he thinks what's yours is his, then why would he light a fire at the coffee shop?"

"It's not about the shop. It's just another way for him to show that he can get to me."

"We need to call Knox in the morning. Show him this note and tell him about what happened at the carnival and our suspicions that Lyle started the fire."

"I don't know. It's just going to make him even more angry, and I don't know what he'll do next."

Mack couldn't help thinking about all the things that had happened the day before as he and Zeus rode the fence line the following morning. He'd stayed the night, but slept on the sofa, not wanting to presume anything with Lorna, but needing to be there in case Lyle showed up in the middle of the night.

He was a little frustrated that it had taken so long for Lorna to show him the note. He understood, and they'd had a lot going on that day, but he wanted her to trust him.

Although he'd kept a secret from her as well. And he didn't want to mention it until he knew if it amounted to anything.

All the talk about the moo monitors and cameras at supper the other night had given him the idea to plant one of the extra wildlife cameras in the alley behind the shop. After Lorna had taken the kids home after school the day before, he'd driven through the alley and hid the camera behind a potted plant where it would be able to capture any activity by the door. He'd hoped to catch Lyle in the act if he tried to break in again, but now he hoped it would show him who had started the fire.

He didn't want to tell Lorna, or Knox, until after he'd had a chance to look at the footage. The camera had still been in place when they'd been there the night before, and he'd shoved it in the pocket of his jacket while Lorna was inside.

He'd planned to check the SD card when he got back to the ranch and had access to his laptop, but Duke was worried that a couple of cows had gotten out and needed him to run fence in the east pasture right away.

He spotted a downed area of fencing and swung off his horse to check it out. It was the only place he'd seen so far, and it didn't look too bad. He shrugged off his flannel shirt—it was close to eight and the sun was already warming the day—and took his tools and some wire from his saddlebag.

They'd posted a sign on the door the night before that the shop wouldn't be open until nine this morning, just to give Lorna a little more time to sleep and not have to rush in after everything that had happened with the fire. So, even with the repair, he figured he'd still have time to check the footage when he got home and if he found something to take it in to show Lorna before she left for the shop.

Everything that *could* go wrong *had* gone wrong that morning. Or maybe Lorna was just cranky because Mack had slept on the sofa the night before—*like a gentleman*—and hadn't tried to sneak into her room. Or her bed.

Although, she *was* glad he had stayed. As much as she wanted to be able to protect herself, it still made her feel safer to know he was in the house.

Max had almost cried this morning when he woke up to find that she'd brought the little scruffy stray dog home.

"I got a puppy and a cow all in the same week," he went around the house yelling. "I love my life."

She'd been thrilled to see the way the dog had taken to her son, cuddling up in his lap and following him around the room, but the animal had still added extra time challenges to her morning with taking her outside, watching that she didn't escape the yard, and setting her up with makeshift bowls of food and water. Thankfully, she already had a bag of dog food since she'd been feeding her at the shop for weeks.

Izzy had been up early and was already fussing, so she tucked her into the swing in the corner of the living room and ran into the kitchen to pack a quick lunch. Gertie was coming over to watch the kids that day, and she usually showed up a few minutes early. Lorna checked her watch. Ten minutes to nine.

She needed to hustle if she was going to get to the shop before it opened.

She heard the front door open.

"Gertie, thank goodness you're here," she said, pulling her hair into a ponytail as she walked into the living room.

But it wasn't Gertie looming over Izzy as she swung back and forth in the swing.

Lyle turned to her, a familiar evil smile she recognized creasing his face, the one that had terror seizing her stomach and bile rising in her throat.

Chapter Twenty-Four

LORNA TRIED TO keep the fear and the tremble out of her voice. "What are you doing here, Lyle?"

He narrowed his eyes as he took a step toward her, and she automatically took a step back. "It seems we have a few things to talk about, sweetie. Like why you called the cops on me. That was pretty embarrassing to have them show up at my front door."

She'd heard he'd been staying out at Misty's trailer on her family's property, so technically they'd shown up at Misty's front door.

"You know we have a rule about talking to the police," he continued, advancing toward her.

"I'm sorry," she said, the words reflexively coming out of her mouth. "It won't happen again."

"Oh, I know it won't." He kicked Max's checkerboard across the floor, breaking the cardboard and sending pieces flying. "Because I'm getting the hell out of this shitty town. Just as soon as you give me what I want." His gaze was greedy as it raked over her body.

Her stomach pitched.

Max came running into the room, the little dog cradled in his arms but pulled up short when he saw Lyle. "Mommy?"

"It's okay, honey. Your daddy just stopped by for a visit. Why don't you take Mocha into the kitchen and get a snack." She prayed he would go. She couldn't bear it if her son was in the room while her husband tried to rape her.

"He doesn't need to leave," Lyle said. "In fact, maybe he should stay. Yeah, I've missed this kid. I've been thinking we should spend some more time together. Maybe *all* our time together."

Panic gripped her chest as if her heart were being squeezed in a vise. "What are you talking about? I thought you said you were leaving town."

"I am. I hate this place. But I need money. And a lot of it to be able to leave and set up a new life somewhere else. I'm thinking maybe a little place on the beach in Florida."

She didn't understand what he was getting at. "That sounds great. You've always liked the ocean."

"Yeah, I have. But like I said, I need money if I'm going to leave. And you're going to give it to me."

"Me? I don't have any money. I'm barely scraping by with what I make at the shop." That queasy feeling in her stomach came back again, and she gulped air to keep from vomiting.

She finally got it.

She knew what he wanted.

That evil grin was back, and he waggled his eyebrows at her. "Now you're getting it. You *do* have something. Something worth a hell of a lot of money.

And I've been telling you that what's yours is mine. So, now I'm here to collect."

"I...I can't just give you my coffee shop. My grandmother left it to me. It was my only inheritance. And besides, you don't even know how to make coffee."

His eyes narrowed again. "Don't sass-talk me. I don't need to make coffee. I'm gonna sell all that coffee shit and every piece of furniture and inventory. With that, and the sale of the building, I should be set."

"I'm not just going to *give* you my shop."

He clamped a hand down on Max's shoulder. "Yes, you are. Either that, or I'll take the kids."

Acid burned her throat, and she pressed her hand to her mouth. "You can't..."

"Oh, but I can. It's my right at any time to fight for custody. Especially when you've proven to be such a bad mom."

"Bad mom?"

"Just since I've been back, I've heard how you were falling down drunk at your sister's wedding while your baby was with a sitter at the emergency room. And it wasn't smart to leave all those flammable things right outside the door of the shop. That's dangerous. And poor Max, you just took him into the doctor for a split lip."

"He fell at the park. You were there."

"Yeah, I was. But, it's still your word against mine. I remember you smacking him for talking back to you."

The panic was rising, and she clasped her trembling hands together. "No one will believe you."

He gave her a pitying look. "Unlike you, I've got

friends in this town. Like Judge Buckner, who I helped with that big insurance claim when his boat got damaged."

More like when he'd gotten drunk and driven it into the dock. But Lyle *had* helped him. And the judge might feel like he owed him.

She needed to think. She needed him out of her house and away from her kids.

"Fine. I'll give you the shop. But in exchange, you have to sign away the rights to the kids."

He chuckled, but in a villainous tone. "I love how you think you have any negotiating power. I'm not asking or bartering or exchanging anything. I'm *taking* the shop. And if you wanna keep arguing with me, I'll take the shop *and* the kids."

"No," she cried, knowing in her heart he would win in the end. He always did. "You can have the shop. It's yours." She knew what he liked and when it came to her children, her pride didn't matter. She fell to her knees before him. "Please Lyle, I'm begging for you not to take the kids."

"That's more like it. And we're going to do it *now*. Just to make sure you don't have time to change your mind or try to get your boyfriend involved."

"Now?"

"Yeah, I Googled how to transfer ownership of a business, and you just have to sign the deed over to me and it's done."

Could it really be that easy to lose her business and her entire livelihood?

"I'm sorry. I don't have the original deed here. I only have a copy. It's a commercial property so they have it on file at the courthouse."

"I know that. I'm not an idiot. They keep them at the Clerk and Recorder's office. Which is where we're going now. They open at nine."

Her shoulders sagged. He *was* an idiot.

But he also had her trapped. And her kids meant more to her than anything else in the world. She would do anything for them. Including giving up the property her grandmother had left her.

She could always get another job. But she couldn't live without her kids. And she would die before she let Lyle take them away from her.

"Okay, I'll go with you. My sitter should be here any minute." She glanced at the clock. It was almost nine. Gertie should have been here by now. She pulled her phone from her pocket. "I just need to call her to make sure she's on her way."

Lyle slapped the phone from her hand, and it went flying across the floor and landed under the corner of the sofa. "You don't need to call anyone. They'll be fine." He shoved Max toward the sofa and pointed at Izzy, who was sound asleep in the swing. "The baby's asleep, and Max is old enough to be able to stay by himself for five minutes." He glared down at her as Max clambered away, hiding himself and the dog behind the arm of the couch. "You can't trick me. I know you're up to something trying to make a phone call."

"No. I swear I'm not. I just don't want to leave my kids all by themselves."

She wasn't expecting the slap as he backhanded her across the face. Pain exploded in her cheek, and tears stung her eyes. She raised her hands in defense, cowering back.

He grabbed her by the ponytail and yanked at her hair. "They're *my* kids, too. And I say they're fine. So, get your fucking purse. We're leaving. Now."

She bit back a sob, not wanting to give him the satisfaction of hearing her cry as he dragged her across the floor by the ponytail. He picked up her crossbody and threw it at her, the clasp of it catching her lip before falling into her lap.

She heard Max crying from behind the sofa and tried to make her tone light. "It's okay, Maxxie. Mommy's just gonna take a little ride with daddy. Gertie will be here any minute. You watch your sister. I love you."

Lyle yanked her to her feet and wrapped his arm around her, gripping her by the forearm as he guided her toward his car.

Gotta keep up appearances. In case any of the neighbors looked out the window. Make it look like they were just a sweet couple walking across the lawn.

Her gaze cast up and down the street, searching for signs of Gertie's car or the woman walking down the sidewalk, but she was nowhere in sight.

Lorna prayed for her children's safety as Lyle opened the car door and shoved her inside.

Chapter Twenty-Five

Mack stuck his foot in the stirrup and swung up into the saddle. He patted Zeus's neck. "Let's go home, boy."

It felt good to say that. And the Lassiter Ranch really did feel like his home now. But he was starting to feel like his home might be in another place as well—with Lorna and the kids. Being with them just felt easy, right, and he was happy when he was around them.

He let out a sigh as Zeus plodded toward the ranch. In his experience, just about the time he was starting to feel happy was when the rug got pulled out from under him.

His phone buzzed, and he pulled it from his pocket to see a FaceTime request from Lorna. He was already smiling when he accepted the call, thinking she'd get a kick out of talking to him while he was out riding his horse. "Good morning, beautiful. Do you miss me already?"

Max's terrified face filled the screen.

"Hey buddy, what's going on?" he asked, already

spurring the horse to move faster as panic tightened his chest.

The boy's bottom lip trembled, and Mack could tell from his red eyes that he'd been crying. "My daddy was here, and he took my mommy."

"What do you mean *took* her?"

"He said he was taking her to the courthouse to see the clerk and re-order."

The clerk and recorder?

"Why?"

"He told my mommy he wants her coffee shop, and she said she would give it to him."

"Where are you? And where is Izzy?"

Max turned the phone to show the baby asleep in the swing behind him then brought it back to his face. "Gertie is supposed to be coming. But she's not here yet. And I don't know what to do."

"You did exactly the right thing, buddy," Mack told him. "And I'm on my way to you right now. But I'm on my horse, and I need you to hang tight while I get back to the barn and to my truck. Can you just stay on the phone with me? And stay right there next to your sister?"

"Yes."

"Okay, hang tight." He gripped the phone tighter then pushed the horse into a full gallop, racing across the field and into the barn. "You still with me, Max?" he called out. He heard a small voice say "yes" as he tucked the phone into his front pocket then frantically pulled off the saddle and bridle, latching Zeus in his stall and sprinting toward his truck.

As soon as he was inside, he pulled his phone back out and was relieved to see Max still sitting in the same space. "I'm in my truck. I'll be there in three minutes. You doin' okay?"

"Yeah. Mocha is here too." He tipped the phone to show the dog curled in his lap.

"I'm glad. You keep petting Mocha and letting your sister sleep. You're doing an amazing job. I'm really proud of you, and I'm so glad you called me."

"Me too."

"Hey Max, why do you have your mom's phone?"

"Because my daddy hit it out of her hand when she tried to call Gertie. Then they left without it, so I used it to call you."

His fingers curled tighter around the steering wheel. He was going to kill that son-of-a-bitch. "That was a really smart thing to do," he said, keeping the focus on the boy's clever actions instead of the violent ones of his father.

He kept up an easy conversation with the boy as he sped into town and practically jumped the curb pulling into the driveway. Max was sitting on the floor by the corner of the sofa when Mack flung open the door, but he got up when he saw him, ran across the room, and flung himself into his arms.

Mack wrapped him up tight, pressing his cheek to the boy's head and thanking God for protecting him and Izzy while they were on their own.

An undercurrent of dread filled him as he thought about what was happening with Lorna, but he knew her well enough to know she'd want him to take care of her kids first before worrying about trying to find her.

The door opened behind him, and he turned to see Gertie coming in.

"My word, I'm so sorry I'm late. I had a flat tire, and I had to wait for the garage to come out and help me, and my stupid phone was dead." She paused in the process of dumping her purse and knitting bag on the table then her expression turned to concern as she must have noticed Max's tear-stained face and the way he was holding on so tightly to Mack. "What's going on? What's happened?"

"My daddy came over and took my mommy," Max told her. "She tried to get him to wait for you, but he said no, so I called Mack on her phone all by myself."

Gertie's eyes widened in alarm. "What?"

"It sounds like Lyle took Lorna to the courthouse to get her to sign over the coffee shop to him," Mack explained.

"Why would she do that?"

"Because my daddy said he would take me and Izzy away if she didn't."

That bastard.

"Oh my gosh, I'm so sorry I was late," Gertie fretted. "I can't believe today of all days…"

"It's okay, it wasn't your fault. It was all Lyle's." He didn't want to think about how terrified Lorna must have been to leave her babies alone. "And apparently, our sweet girl has slept through the whole ordeal." Mack nodded to Izzy as he gently set the boy down on the sofa. The little dog jumped up and curled into his lap. "Now that Gertie's here, I'm going to go find your mom, okay?"

Max nodded.

Gertie hustled to the sofa, sat down, and pulled the boy to her side. "Should I call the police?"

"No, not yet. We've already been talking to a deputy. Let me find Lorna, and then we'll call him."

"Go," Gertie told him. "I've got the kids covered. Go get Lorna."

"You don't have to hold onto me so tight," Lorna told Lyle as he all but dragged her into the courthouse, using the same tight controlling grasp on her forearm he'd used before. She'd snuck a glance at her arm in the car and saw the set of circular bruises the grips of his fingers had left there. "I'm not going anywhere."

"I just don't want you changing your mind and trying to run away."

"I won't change my mind. My kids are more important to me than anything. So, you can have the coffee shop and the building."

He leaned close to her ear. "I know I can."

He was close enough for her to smell the beer on his breath, and she wondered if that was from this morning already or the stale leftover scent of the night before. Alcohol was the usual culprit fueling the worst of his rages, and she worried about what it could talk him into this morning.

The Clerk and Recorder's office was on the second floor at the end of the hall. Lorna was thankful the elevator and hallway had been empty, and they hadn't run into anyone they knew.

They stopped outside the office door, and Lyle tightened his hold on her arm. "Now, I'm gonna let you go, but you're gonna behave when we get in there, right?"

"Yes," she whispered, loathing the submission in her voice.

She wanted to yell and scream and fight and claw his psychotic eyes out, but more than anything, she wanted to get this over with and get back to her children.

Please God, let Gertie have shown up already.

They stepped through the office door, and Lorna was both thankful and mortified to see Judy Fitzgerald sitting at her desk. She was grateful for the familiar face of a friend, but ashamed that this woman would soon witness how weak she was and how she had succumbed to Lyle's power over her.

Judy looked up, a pleasant smile on her face as they walked in, but her smile faltered as her gaze dropped to the bruises on Lorna's arm.

She hadn't seen her reflection, but she wondered if the red sting of the backhand still showed on her face, as well. Maybe the heat of humiliation rushing to her cheeks would hide it.

"Lorna. Lyle. What can I help you with today?" Judy kept her tone congenial, ever the professional.

Lyle nudged Lorna hard in the ribs.

"Oh…um…we would…I mean…*I* would like the deed to the commercial building where Mountain Brew is located because we…I mean…*I* want to transfer ownership of it over to Lyle."

"You want to *give* the coffee shop to *him*?" Judy asked, the astonishment evident in her eyes.

Lyle nudged her already bruised ribs again, and she fought not to cry out in pain. "Yes, I do."

"I don't think it's *your* job to question your

customers, *Ju-*dy," Lyle sneered. "I think it's your job to just get them what the hell they want."

Lyle's behavior was terrifying Lorna. He usually used his charm and charisma to get his way with people. In this town, he was one of the good old boys, a high school jock, who liked to pick up a round at the bar. But today, the asshole that she knew and had once loved was surfacing, and it told her that he'd either already been drinking or just how desperate he was.

And neither option was a good one.

Judy peered at Lyle over the top of her glasses. "I see. Thank you for explaining that part of my job to me. Unfortunately, I'm not going to be able to help you today."

Lyle glared at her. "Why not?"

"Because we don't keep those deeds on file here. There was a fire some years ago that destroyed a bunch of records, and ever since then, we have stored the most important documents in Denver."

"So, you're saying we have to drive all the way down the pass and to Denver?"

"No, not necessarily. I can put in a request for the documents, and they'll get sent up here, usually within five to seven business days."

"Five to seven days? We can't wait that long." He peered around the office at the filing cabinets and shelves behind her desk. "You've got to have some kind of transfer of ownership form we can sign to do this today. I looked it up online, and it said we just had to come down to the clerk and recorder and you could take care of it."

Judy looked at Lorna. "Are you sure this is what you really want to do?"

"Of course it is," Lyle answered for her. "It's part of our divorce settlement. Now are you gonna help us with this, or am I gonna have to find someone else who can?"

"No," Judy said, staring directly at Lorna and giving her a solemn nod. "I can help you." She opened a file drawer, rifled through it, then drew out a one-page form. "This should accomplish what you need until the deed arrives. It's a transfer of business but it takes two business days to take effect. So, with the weekend, the business won't become yours until Monday." She smiled at Lyle, but the smile didn't quite meet her eyes. "Surely, you can wait through the weekend to take over the shop."

"I guess I'll have to," Lyle said. "Where do we sign?"

"Let me get a little information from you." She filled out their full names and the address of the business then frowned. "I just realized, we're going to need a notary to sign this, and she doesn't come in till later today. So, you may just have to come back."

Lorna finally caught on. Bless this woman for trying to help her.

"That's ridiculous. You can witness it and have her put her little stamp on it when she comes in later," Lyle told her, snatching the form from her hand and signing the line by his name without even reading it.

Lorna was pretty sure that wasn't how it worked, but if it would get them out of there quicker, she'd sign it. Lyle thrust the pen into her hand, and she scribbled her name on the line.

"I'm sure that will be fine," Judy told them as she

took the form back. "And I'll place an order for the deed to be delivered up here as soon as possible. Is there anything else I can help with?"

"No, that's it." Lyle plucked one of the cards from the holder on her desk and scribbled his name and number on it. "Call *me* as soon as it comes in."

"I look forward to it," Judy said, but Lorna caught the sarcasm in her voice.

Lyle was too busy shoving her out the door to notice. She was sure the opinion of an older woman in a county office was of no consequence to her arrogant ex-husband.

The elevator at the end of the hallway dinged, and tears sprang to her eyes as the doors opened and she saw Mack inside.

His jaw was set, and the heels of his cowboy boots struck the tile flooring as he strode out of the elevator and toward them.

The door to the stairwell was in front of them, and Lyle grabbed her arm and pushed her through. She stumbled down one flight in front of him, then he shoved her to the corner of the landing, and she fell to her knees as he sprinted down the next flight without her. "I'll see you soon," he called over his shoulder. "And tell Lassiter to back the fuck off."

The door at the top of the landing banged open, and Mack flew down the steps and gathered her into his arms.

She pushed against him. "I've got to get home. The kids are alone."

"I just left your house. Gertie's with them."

Her knees buckled, but Mack's strong arms held her up, and the sobs she'd been holding in finally broke free. She clung to his chest, surrendering to his caring embrace as he hugged her to him.

"I was so worried about you," he said into her hair. "I was praying I would find you here before that asshole took you somewhere else."

"How did you find me?"

"Max used your phone and Face Timed me out at the ranch."

A laugh broke through her tears. "Of course he did."

"You would have been so proud of him. He sat right next to the swing, and Izzy slept the entire time it took me to get to him. Which I'm pretty sure I set a new record for speeding to your house."

"What happened to Gertie?"

"She had a flat tire and a dead phone. She feels terrible for being late."

"Oh no, poor thing."

He drew back and wiped the tears from her cheeks then brushed her hair back from her forehead and pressed a kiss there. "Max said Lyle hurt you. Are you okay?"

She nodded, touched by his deep concern. "Yeah, I'm fine. He caught me off guard, and Max saw him backhand me, but he could have done a lot worse." She told him about Lyle's threats to take the kids and his claims of her being a bad mother.

"That's bullshit. You're a great mom. You always put your kids first."

"Thank you. And I would do *anything* for my kids. That's why I'm giving him the shop."

"He can't just expect you to *give* him a commercial property."

"Oh, yes, he can. That's why he brought me down here, to transfer ownership of the building to him."

"Did you do it?"

"Yes, I think so. Judy Fitzgerald helped us, and she said the actual deed was in Denver and it would take close to a week to get here, but we did sign something that said he gets the shop in two business days."

"That gives us the weekend to figure out how to fight him and to keep your kids."

She shook her head as she pulled away. "No. I'm not going to fight him. He can have the building. Especially if it means he'll go away. He wants to take the money from the sale and start over in Florida. I can always find another job."

"But that coffee shop was your dream."

"And I got to enjoy that dream for a little while. But nothing outranks my kids. And it will be worth the loss if he leaves."

"Guys like that have a way of showing back up again. Especially if they think they can get something out of you again."

"This is what I can do now." She swiped the remaining tears from her cheeks with the back of her hand. "Can you give me a ride back to my house now? I'd really like to hug my kids."

Chapter Twenty-Six

"Mommy!" Max cried and ran across the room to fling himself into Lorna's arms when she and Mack walked into the house five minutes later. "Mack found you. Are you okay?"

"Yes, I'm fine," she said, planting kisses all over his face. "And I heard you were very brave and did a great job taking care of your sister."

He pushed her hair away from her ear to whisper into it. "I was pretty scared, Mommy."

She hugged him tighter. "I know you were, honey. I was, too. But we're okay now, and we're gonna be just fine."

"I'm so sorry I wasn't here earlier," Gertie said, drying her hands on a dish towel as she walked in from the kitchen.

"It's okay," Lorna told her. "It wasn't your fault."

Gertie shrugged and jerked her thumb back to the kitchen. "I'm making your favorite—homemade chicken and noodles with mashed potatoes—to make up for it. It'll be ready when you get home from work, and there will be enough to share." She gave a not-so-subtle nod in Mack's direction.

"That's kind of you, Gertie, but not necessary. You do plenty of things to help me already."

"I'd like to offer to help, too," Mack said. "Why don't you let me go into the shop so you can stay home and just be with the kids. You said Emily is coming in today. Between the two of us, we can take care of things."

"That's a good idea," Gertie agreed. "And I'll stick around to make lunch so you can take a nap, too."

Lorna glanced from one to the other as Max took off to play with the dog. "I feel like you two are somehow in cahoots with this 'let's be nice to Lorna' business." She rolled her shoulders against the stiffness and pain in her back and ribs. "But I learned as a single mom, to never say no to someone's offer of help. So, I will take you both up on it."

Gertie gave her a hug, then jerked back as Lorna winced at the pain in her ribs. "Why don't you head upstairs and run a hot bath, and I'll bring you a cup of tea and an ice pack for that cheek."

Mack's expression hardened as Gertie headed into the kitchen. "I'd like to go find that little turd and beat the hell out of him for you."

She laughed then winced again. "I'd like that too, but it won't help anything."

"All I want to do is help you," he said, gently putting his arms around her. "What I really want to do is go all caveman and pack you and the kids and that scruffy little dog into my truck and take you back to the ranch where I know you'll be safe. But I know you well enough by now to know that you probably wouldn't go, and what you'd really appreciate the most is for me to march down to Mountain Brew and make macchiatos and serve up some warm cinnamon scones."

She grinned up at him. "Which is almost as manly as that caveman idea." She sighed and pressed her good cheek to his chest. "I'm tempted by the idea though. But I don't think you need to worry about the 'little turd'. He got what he wanted, so I don't think I'll see him again until we hear back from Judy that the paperwork went through, and he shows up for the keys to the building."

Mack's hands curled into fists. "Can't I hurt him just a little bit?"

She hugged him tighter. "No, but thanks for wanting to."

"You want me to call one of my brothers or Duke to come over, just to be a presence at the house?"

She shook her head. "No. Gertie will be here, and I really don't expect him to come back today."

"Any chance you have a gun in the house?"

"Hell no. What I do have is *kids* in the house. So, I don't need or want a firearm. And I'm not good enough with one to be able to confidently use it anyway. I'm afraid if I tried to, someone would just take it away and use it on me."

And by someone, she meant her ex-husband. She'd always been thankful he wasn't much a gun guy. Things could have gone much worse for her if he had been.

Mack frowned. "I get your point. But you might be the only single woman in Colorado not to have a handgun and their concealed permit."

"I'm fine with that distinction." She gently pushed him toward the door. "Now, will you please go make some frappucinos. And don't worry, Emily can practically run the shop on her own, so just do whatever she tells you to do. And please tell her *thank you* and that I'm sorry for sending a cowboy to make coffee, but you're cute, so that should make up for it."

Lorna jerked awake, the image of a broken and bloody Mack still in her mind's eye. Bleary-eyed and disoriented, she tried to catch her breath as she untangled her legs from the sheets on her bed.

How long had she been out? She'd only meant to close her eyes for a few minutes.

She found her phone next to her pillow and was surprised to see she'd been asleep for almost two hours. The trauma of the morning must have gotten to her more than she'd thought, and her body had retreated into sleep. The sleep she could use, the nightmare of Lyle trying to kill Mack, not so much.

She tried to push the dream from her mind. Lyle had been a defensive end in high school, but he didn't often pick fights with other men. Not when he had his own personal punching bag at home. So, she didn't imagine he'd try to start something with Mack, but she also knew her ex-husband liked to fight dirty.

After taking a few minutes to wash her face and clean the smudges of mascara from under her eyes, she walked down the stairs to find Max and Mocha tucked into one corner of the sofa and Gertie and her latest knitting project in the other. Izzy was on a blanket in the middle of the floor, enclosed in a fort of pillows. An episode of Bluey was on the television, and they all appeared to be watching it.

"Oh, you're up," Gertie said, setting down her knitting. "How was your nap? I checked on you once, and you were out cold."

"A bit groggy, if I'm honest. I'm all about the fifteen-minute power nap, but I'm not sure passing out for two hours in the middle of the afternoon is a great idea for me."

"I made a fresh batch of chocolate chip cookies, and there's some iced tea in the fridge," Gertie said. "Do you want me to make you a glass?"

Lorna shook her head. "No, you've done enough for today. Why don't you go home?"

Gertie raised an eyebrow. "And miss this episode of Bluey? I think not. Plus, I was hoping you'd invite me to stick around for supper."

"Yes, of course you can stay, if you want to. I just don't want to overstep."

"No such thing when it comes to family. And that's how I've come to think of you and these sweet babies."

"In that case, please don't ever leave us."

She and Gertie laughed as Max waved his hand in their direction.

"Shh. You're missing the show," he said, not taking his attention from the screen.

Lorna squeezed in between him and Gertie, pulling her son into her lap and cuddling him and the puppy as they all finished watching the show together.

Mack showed up around five, just in time to help set the table. He and Max both had second helpings, and he couldn't stop telling Gertie her chicken and noodles were the best he'd ever had.

He helped clear the table and load the dishwasher, and Lorna noticed that Max had started doing the same after watching Mack's actions the last few times he'd been there for a meal.

"You got a few minutes to talk?" Mack asked her after the dishes were done and Gertie had gone home. They were sitting in the swing together on the back porch watching Max run around the yard with the little dog.

"Sure." There was something she wanted to talk to him about too. She'd been thinking about it all afternoon. The nightmare had really shaken her, and she would never forgive herself if Mack got hurt because of something her idiot ex did.

The only thing that made sense to her was for them to back off and stop acting like they were a couple. Especially, if it only antagonized Lyle.

Mack was so protective of her and the kids, and there was part of her that loved that, but another part of her knew he didn't understand her willingness to give up the shop and that she needed to handle this Lyle business on her own.

But she'd let Mack talk first, before she brought up the idea that she expected she'd be getting some resistance to.

"I want to talk to you, too," she said. "But you go first."

He gave her a questioning look but then forged on. "So, I took a liberty and did something this afternoon, and I wanted to tell you about it."

She raised her eyebrows. "Did it involve beating up my ex-husband?"

"I wish," Mack said. "But no, it's nothing that sinister."

"Okay, go ahead."

"I noticed a burnt-out light bulb in your office at the shop, so I stopped at the hardware store on my way in to pick up a new package of them. And I saw they had one of those security camera setups on sale—the kind you hook to an app on your phone—so I picked it up for you." He held his hand up to her protest. "I'm pretty sure I can counter all your objections, and also, I already set it up this afternoon. There were only four cameras that came with it, and I strategically placed three of them in the lobby and one in your office."

She let out a sigh. "I appreciate the thought, but one, you shouldn't have spent that kind of money on me, and two, the shop might belong to Lyle after this weekend."

"Count it as an early birthday present. And even if The Turd, which, by the way, is what I've decided to call him from now on, does get his hands on the shop, it might not be for weeks, and I'd just feel better knowing the cameras are there."

"I've looked into security cameras before but decided against them because this is Woodland Hills and everyone watches out for each other, *and* because they all needed some kind of paid subscription for them to be online."

"Oh…well…this one came with a free introductory period," he said with a shrug, but didn't meet her eye, which made her wonder if he hadn't footed the bill for that expense too. "Just let me show you how it works. Please?"

She guessed it couldn't hurt. And he'd already spent the money, so might as well take advantage of the service, even if it was short-lived. Maybe Mack could move the system out to the ranch to watch the cows after the shop was gone.

"Fine."

"I set it up on my phone this afternoon," he told her. "Just to make sure it worked, and to accept the terms of the...um...introductory period...but once we get it all set up on your phone, I can disable it on mine."

He showed her how to find the app on her phone and set the notifications to alert her if someone was in the store. "It's motion-sensored," he said. "So, hopefully you won't get any notifications when the shop is closed. But you can also open the app and take a live look around at any time."

She had to admit, it was a pretty neat system. She didn't deem herself very technologically savvy, but it seemed easy enough that even she could understand how to work it.

"Thank you," she told him. "This was really thoughtful. And it would be a great idea if I were keeping the shop."

"There's something else."

"Ohhh-kay."

"These aren't the only cameras I set up."

"What do you mean?"

"I got the idea from Dodge the other night when he was showing us the moo monitors. We had an extra wildlife camera, so I set it up in the alley behind your shop the next morning."

It took her a minute, but then she realized what he was saying. "Did it catch Lyle on camera setting the fire?"

Mack sighed. "Not as well as I'd hoped it would. You can see someone back there, and it looks like they are pouring something on the ground. But the person is wearing a hoodie pulled up over their head, and the picture is pretty grainy. I wanted you to look at it and see if you could see anything distinguishing that could tie it to Lyle, then we could give it to Knox."

She pulled in a breath. "Okay, so I love the way you were trying to catch the culprit behind the break-in, and the footage *could* help prove it wasn't me if Lyle decides to pursue this idea that I'm a bad mom…"

"Which is garbage."

"Thank you. But my point is, Lyle is already pissed off about me talking to the cops…"

"That's his problem."

She sighed. "But that's the thing. He has a way of making *his* problems, *my* problems." She sighed again, this one even heavier than the first. "Which leads me to what I wanted to talk to you about."

"Okay."

"So, first I want to thank you for everything you've done for me the past week. You have been there for me like no one, other than my sister, ever has. And I love seeing you and hanging out with you—honestly, I never get tired of being with you—but still, I think we need to cool things off."

Mack cocked an eyebrow. "I'm not sure how the

first things you said—about me being there for you and how you love hanging out with me—correlate with that last thing you just said."

"I know. I'm doing a bad job of explaining it, but I just don't want you to get hurt."

And she didn't want *herself* to get hurt.

She was starting to like this guy, and to depend on him, *too much*. If…when…he left—which they always left—she, and her kids, would be devastated.

"Hurt? You mean by The Turd? I'm not afraid of him. I'm waiting, no, *begging*, for him to come at me. I can't wait to show him the way a backhand to the face, then a roundhouse to the head, feels."

"This is what I'm talking about. I don't want you to have to fight Lyle for me."

"Not *have* to…*get* to."

"I'm serious. He's dangerous, and I won't have you putting yourself at risk for me. I don't need you to be my hero."

His expression clouded. "I already told you that just because I ride a white horse, to not expect me to be a conquering hero. I'm *not* hero material, and I've never been anyone's knight in shining armor. That's not what I was trying to do. I've told you before how amazing and brave I think you are, and I've always tried to encourage you to be your own hero."

"Thank you. I appreciate that. And I want to be. But I can't if you're always stepping in and trying to save me. I know you don't understand my decision to give up the shop, and I just can't keep defending that decision to you. I have to do what I think is right for me and my kids. You said above all else we were friends, so I need you to be my friend now, and give me some space to deal with my ex-husband. On my own."

"Are you serious?" The light banter was gone, replaced with confusion and hurt. "Lorna, we *were* friends, *are* friends, but I thought we…"

He wasn't getting it.

"No, you thought wrong. This is not what I want. Or what I need. I got carried away. I let things get too intimate. I crossed the line, and I'm sorry." She could see the pain in his eyes, the way he kept flinching, as if her words were cutting him to the quick. She felt like an inept surgeon, slicing off pieces of this sweet man's heart.

And that was the problem too. Mack was sweet and kind and thoughtful. He was someone she could really fall for.

Who was she kidding? She'd already fallen. Hard.

But she couldn't afford to fall for someone. Not now. Maybe not ever. She had her kids to focus on. Her business. Or getting a job, now that her business was gone.

"There's nothing to be sorry for," he said. "I was there too."

"Yes, well, spending a few nights in bed together doesn't mean you get to decide things in my life."

"I was trying to help."

"I don't want your help. That's what I'm trying to tell you. You're acting like we're a real couple, and we're *not*."

Those were the words that finally did it, that shut the light completely down in his eyes.

His shoulders sagged, and she could almost see the defensive walls go shooting up around him.

"No, I guess not." He pushed up from the swing. "I'll get out of your way then." He turned and strode away, cutting through the yard between her house and her neighbor's.

She wanted to call his name, to tell him she didn't mean it, and to have him come back and put his arms around her again. Because in his arms had been the only place that had felt right the past several days. The only place she felt like she could breathe. Or laugh. Or cry.

The only place she could truly feel safe to just be herself.

And now she had pushed him away.

She knew she was doing it to protect him. The dream she'd had that afternoon had felt like a premonition, and she couldn't allow it to come true—couldn't forgive herself if she let Lyle do anything to harm Mack.

But in her heart, she knew she was breaking it off now, before they got even closer, to protect herself, too.

It was almost nine that night when Lorna went into the kitchen to make a cup of tea. She'd gotten both kids to bed almost an hour ago, then put on her most comfy pajama pants and a soft faded T-shirt and tried to read then watch some television. But she couldn't focus on her book or pay attention to a show.

Her heart was aching, and she kept second-guessing her decision to push Mack away. She knew it was the right thing to do, to protect him, and to keep her from getting too close then having another man in her life leave her. And her kids. But it still hurt.

A knock sounded at the front door, and she let out a small yelp as she jumped. She heard the doorknob jiggle.

Someone was trying to get into her house.

Chapter Twenty-Seven

Lorna's whole body tensed. She looked around the kitchen for a weapon and grabbed the biggest knife from the block on the counter.

Inching into the living room, her whole body on alert as she strained to listen for the intruder's next move.

She jumped again as a knock sounded on the front window then she sagged in relief as she saw Maisie's face peering in. Her friend's eyes went wide as she saw the knife clutched in Lorna's hands.

"Oh my gosh, I'm so sorry we scared you," Maisie said when Lorna opened the front door.

"Nice knife," Dodge said, peering at her over Maisie's shoulder.

"What are you doing here?"

"We...um...heard about what happened today, and we wanted to come over and check on you," Maisie said.

Lorna looked at the tote bag and duffle on the porch by their feet. "And did checking on me mean spending the night?"

"Well, we just thought that—"

"Mack called you, didn't he?" she said, interrupting her friend before she made things worse with another lame excuse.

"Yes," Dodge admitted. "But we were worried about you guys, too. And we would all just feel better if you let us sleep on your floor tonight. Just in case the douche-nugget decides to stop by."

Lorna opened the door wider to let them in. "I get it. You can sleep in Leni's room. There's wedding stuff piled in the chair, but the sheets on the bed are clean."

"We won't get in your way." Dodge gave her a quick hug before heading toward the kitchen where she heard him check to make sure the back door was locked.

"Do you want to talk about it? Or anything?" Maisie asked.

Lorna shook her head. "Not really. I'm honestly just exhausted. I was just making some tea then I was going to bed."

"Okay, Dodge and I will make sure everything is locked up down here. Don't worry about us. I know where everything is. Good night."

Both Maisie and Elizabeth had slept over after late night margarita parties, and Lorna trusted her friend could take care of getting herself and Dodge to bed.

She was exhausted, but an hour later, she still couldn't fall asleep. She'd tried counting sheep as she'd lay in bed and listened to the sounds of Maisie and Dodge coming up the stairs and the water running and toilet flushing in Leni's bathroom. She'd tried counting backwards from one hundred to one, then again in multiples of seven. She tried relaxing her whole body, starting with her toes and working up to her ears.

Nothing worked.

She couldn't get Mack Lassiter and the hurt in his eyes—hurt she'd put there—out of her mind.

Her phone buzzed in the charger on her nightstand, and her heart leapt as she hoped it was a text from Mack. Maybe he was texting to check on her or tell her goodnight or that he couldn't sleep either.

But when she picked up her phone, there weren't any notifications of new text messages.

Then why had it buzzed?

It vibrated again in her hand, and a notification popped up from the new app she'd just installed that afternoon. A notification that meant something, or some*one*, had set off the motion sensor in the coffee shop.

She tapped the notification and prayed it was a mouse running across the floor who had set it off as the app opened to the screen showing the lobby of the shop. *And* a man casually walking through the center of the tables.

A man who she used to be married to.

The Little Turd walked up to the counter and checked the drawer of the cash register then grabbed a stack of cups and hurled them through the air.

Seeing him should have made her scared, but this time it just made her mad. *Like really pissed her off.*

How dare he break into her shop and then start destroying her stuff?

She got out of bed and slipped her feet into a pair of sandals laying on the floor by her closet. She opened her bedroom door and crossed the hall to Leni's room to tell Dodge and Maisie what she'd seen.

But, as she approached the slightly open door, she heard Dodge's steady snoring and Maisie's even breathing. She peeked into Max's room and the nursery, and both kids were sound asleep.

She could call the police. Or Mack. He would be in his truck and probably beat her to the coffee shop, even though her house was only a few minutes away.

No, she was sick of being afraid of Lyle Williams.

And she was going to tell him so.

She'd be there and back in ten minutes, she thought as she slipped out of the house and into her car. Plus, the coffee shop was on the main street of town, so there would be plenty of people around if Lyle tried anything.

All she wanted to do was march into the shop, *her* shop, and tell him to get the hell out of it. That it was hers until the paperwork went through.

She had a few other choice words to say to him, but those would suffice for now.

Some of her bravado faded as she pulled up in front of the shop and noticed the street was completely deserted. No cars. No people. No lights on in any of the businesses.

The diner, the Tipsy Pig, and the local bar, where the majority of the people would be, were all on the edge of town, closer to the highway.

Her bravado might have faded, but her anger hadn't.

She got out of the car and faced the shop. Okay, she was pissed, but she wasn't stupid.

And it wasn't his shop *yet*.

She checked the app once more to confirm Lyle

was still in the store, then tapped back to place a call to 9-1-1 to report a break-in.

Then she unlocked the front door to face The Little Turd.

The county sheriff's office was located between Woodland Hills and the next town over of Creedence, so it should take them less than ten minutes to get to her.

Plenty of time for her to finally tell Lyle what she thought of him. And surely, he couldn't do too much to her in that short amount of time.

Knowing he wouldn't be able to sleep anyway, Mack had taken Zeus on a long trail ride through the mountains above the ranch then spent a good hour brushing and grooming him before going back to the house and calling it a night.

Duke had already gone to bed by the time he made it inside, and Maisie had texted him thirty minutes ago to confirm they were sleeping over at Lorna's and that everyone was tucked in for the night.

In his bedroom, he shucked off his clothes then checked his phone, just to make sure Lorna hadn't tried to message him.

Nothing.

Angry, hurt, and frustrated, he took a long shower, running the water as hot as he could stand it, letting it wash over him until the spray turned cold. He dried off then pulled on a pair of sweats, thinking he might go into the kitchen to make a sandwich. If he wasn't going to sleep, might as well eat.

His phone buzzed on his dresser, and he crossed the room, hoping it might be Lorna. But his heart leapt to his throat as he saw several notifications from the security camera app.

He opened the app and swore as he watched that bastard, Lyle, waltzing around Lorna's shop like he already owned the place and making a mess as he knocked things around.

Screw that guy.

This felt like the opportunity he'd been waiting for to give that asshole a piece of his mind. And an even bigger piece of his fists.

He leaned down and grabbed his boots, pulling them on over his sweats, not wanting to take the time to change into jeans in case Lyle left the store and Mack missed his opportunity.

Still watching the screen, he walked to his closet to grab a shirt, but turned in his tracks and started running as he saw Lorna enter the shop and Lyle advance on her.

Mack swore again as that son-of-a-bitch took a swing that sent Lorna flying back into one of the tables.

Duke was standing in the kitchen fixing a cup of tea, and Mack shouted at him as he ran past. "Call 9-1-1! Lyle's at the coffee shop with Lorna, and he's beatin' the hell out of her."

Then he was out the door, soaring off the steps, in his truck, and flying down the highway.

Hang on, baby.

Three minutes.

That was all he would need to make it to the coffee shop. Although, he was trying to make it in two. He pushed his truck, figuring if a cop spotted him doing ninety-five down the highway, he'd just have to chase him straight to the shop.

He still had the app open, and he glanced at the screen, cursing as he saw Lorna throw a cup at, and miss, Lyle. Then he picked it up and flung it back at her, catching her on the side of the arm.

Hold on, darlin'. I'm coming.

Two minutes.

Then he'd make that bastard pay.

Chapter Twenty-Eight

PAIN EXPLODED IN Lorna's face as Lyle's fist collided with her cheekbone.

She cried out in pain as the force of the blow sent her reeling back, and she crashed into one of the tables. The corner of it bit into her hip as she whacked it on her way down.

"Do you think you can come into *my* building and talk to *me* that way?" Lyle shouted, advancing on her again.

She skittered backward, pedaling her body away from him with the heels of her sneakers.

So, in hindsight, it might have been a mistake to march into the shop, loaded for bear, and yell at him to get the hell out of her business. Which she meant in both the literal and figurative sense.

It had been a huge mistake for her to come down here to face Lyle, period.

What the hell had she been thinking?

A coffee mug, one of the many Lyle had been throwing across the lobby, lay within reach, and she grabbed it and hurled it toward his head.

She missed.

He grabbed it and threw it back at her. He might have played defense, but he still knew how to throw, and pain shot through her arm as the cup skimmed past the side of it.

Grabbing the back of a chair, she pulled herself to her feet then pushed the chair between them. "Why can't you just leave me alone?"

He let out a laugh, the evilness in it churning her stomach. "Just because *I* don't want you anymore, doesn't mean anyone else gets to have what will *always* belong to me. And don't you worry, I'm planning to pay Lassiter a visit before I leave town. He doesn't get to make me look like a fool and get away with it."

She laughed, and his head jerked toward her. "Mack didn't have to do anything. You look like a fool all on your own."

She'd *never* laughed at him or talked back to him before.

And the sheer gall of her doing it now was sending him into even more of a rage.

He came charging toward her, and she stumbled back, tripping over the cup, and falling on her butt. She flipped over and got to her knees before he grabbed her ankle and dragged her back toward him.

She screamed as he rolled her over then straddled her body, landing hard on her hips as he sank down to pin her to the floor.

He punched her once, and she tasted blood in her mouth.

Then his hands were around her throat, choking the life from her. She bucked her hips, trying to push him off her.

Blackness clouded the sides of her vision. She was going to pass out.

Then he was going to kill her.

She thought of her precious babies and how stupid she'd been to face him alone.

Then his body was lifted from hers, as if a giant hand had reached down and plucked him into the air then threw him across the room.

She blinked, not quite believing that it was Mack she was seeing, his hair wet, no shirt, his muscles flexed as he tore after Lyle, who lay in a heap on the floor.

Mack grabbed him by the front of his shirt and hauled him up then swung his fist in an arc that slammed into Lyle's nose with a sickening crunch.

Blood ran down Lyle's face. It was bright red against his white teeth as he smiled at Mack. "Come on, Lassiter, she's not worth fighting over. You can have her. All I want is the building."

"Too bad all you're getting is my fist in your mouth." Mack punched him again, the blood on his face spraying across Lyle's yellow T-shirt.

Lyle's arm reached out, found another of the ceramic cups on the floor, and Lorna tried to scream a warning at Mack as he swung his arm up and crashed the cup into the side of Mack's head.

The blow opened a gash on his forehead and appeared to have stunned him. It was enough for Lyle to gain purchase as he pushed Mack off him and scrambled away.

Mack roared after him, but Lyle grabbed a chair and swung it into Mack's midsection. The blow sent him flying back, and he hit the floor.

Then Lyle was on top of him, swinging his fists and screaming with rage as he straddled his body. He used his knees to pin Mack's arms then got his hands around the cowboy's throat, the same way he'd done to her.

Lorna pulled herself up, every breath painful as she pulled it through her bruised throat.

She had to get to Mack. She might not have been strong enough to save herself, but she would find the strength to save the man she loved.

"Stop it. You're killing him," she screamed, dragging herself forward.

"That's the idea," Lyle shouted back, his teeth clenched with the effort of trying to hold Mack down while he strangled his throat.

Lorna used a chair to pull herself to her feet. She saw Mack's body go limp just as she lifted the chair and swung it at Lyle's back. It hit him in the side, and he fell off Mack's chest, grunting in pain as his shoulder hit the ground.

"You bitch!" he screamed, pushing to his knees then his feet and coming at her again. He swung his fist, connected with her jaw, and sent her reeling back.

She fell to the ground and skittered back, her hands behind her, desperately searching for something to throw at him or hit him with.

He picked up the same chair she'd hit him with and raised it over his head as he stalked toward her. Standing above her, he raised the chair higher, poised to slam it into her body.

Then a shot rang out, and a red spot bloomed on his chest as he flew backward and into one of the tables, smacking his head as he fell.

Chapter Twenty-Nine

Lorna turned her head, blinking against the blood dripping into her eye from a cut on her brow, expecting to see a Sheriff's deputy standing there.

Instead, she saw a petite blonde woman, holding a gun outstretched in one hand, while the other hung limp, dangling at her side. Lorna was sure it was Misty, although her face was so swollen and black and purple with bruises, it was almost hard to recognize her.

"Is the fucker dead?" she asked, the words barely audible through her split and swollen lips.

Lorna glanced at Lyle's motionless body as she crawled toward Mack. "I think so."

"Deserves it," Misty murmured as she dropped the gun and slid down the wall and to the floor.

Mack had turned to his side and was holding his throat as he coughed and sucked in gasps of air. Blood dripped from the cut on his forehead, and his lip was swollen and split too. Lorna reached for him, and he pulled her to his body, spooning her protectively against his stomach as he held her close.

"I got you," he gasped.

"I got you, too," she whispered as she clasped his hand tightly to her chest.

Red and blue lights flashed across the wall of the shop as the sounds of engines pulling up to the curb, doors slamming, and boots hitting the sidewalk filled the air.

Then the coffee shop was full of voices as two of the deputies secured Lyle while another one raced to Misty, and another ran to Lorna and Mack.

Sirens wailed and an ambulance pulled up. EMT's rushed inside, trying to triage who needed them the most.

Since Lyle had been shot in the chest, he took priority. Lorna wasn't sure if she was sad or glad when she realized her ex-husband was still alive. She didn't want Misty to go to prison, so she guessed she was glad.

"Take care of Misty first," Lorna told the EMT who approached them. Someone had turned on the overhead lights, and she could see the other woman slumped in a heap by the wall, her injuries even more apparent in the light. "She's in bad shape."

She and Mack were battered and bruised, but the woman who had just saved her life seemed to be hanging on by a thread. Lorna's heart went out to her as she had to assume Lyle had been the one who had beaten her so badly.

"Mack!" Duke's voice rang out as he ran into the shop.

Ford and Dodge burst through the door behind him, and they all three rushed toward them. Duke fell to his knees beside Mack. "You all right, son? What do you need?"

Mack's lip was split and bleeding, and he spit a gob of blood onto the floor. "I'm okay. But I could use a hand gettin' up."

His brother's helped them to get up and then half-carried, half-led them a few feet to the loveseat in front of the window, where they both sank into the cushioned sofa. Duke passed them each a stack of napkins, and Lorna pressed hers to the cut on her brow, while Mack dabbed at his lip then held it to a gaping gash on his forehead. Both his brothers served as volunteer fireman and had first aid training, so Ford looked Mack over while Dodge gingerly checked Lorna.

"Doesn't seem like you have a concussion," Ford told his brother. "But you're gonna feel like you got hit by a truck in the morning."

Dodge grinned. "A Mack truck."

Mack grinned back. "The best kind."

Lorna was glad they were able to tease each other. She wasn't sure if she wanted to laugh or burst into tears but had a feeling she'd be doing a little of both in the next few hours.

They'd already wheeled Lyle out on one of the stretchers, and they had Misty strapped to another one. Lorna pushed to her feet, a little unsteady, but she needed to make sure she was okay.

"Wait," she told the EMT who was pushing the stretcher past them. She leaned over Misty, taking her good hand and gently squeezing it. Tears fell as she took in the carnage that remained of the beautiful woman. "Thank you, Misty," Lorna told her, her words catching on the emotion. "You saved our lives. How did you know he was here?"

"This building and the money he was gonna make from selling it is all he's been talking about," she answered, squeezing Lorna's hand. "I'm sorry, Lorna. I never knew he was like this. He beat the hell out of me and has had me locked in the bedroom of the trailer for days. He was drunk when he left tonight, and didn't get the door all the way latched, so I finally escaped. I got in one of my brother's trucks, and I planned to just keep driving, away from him and this town, then I saw Lyle's car parked in the alley. There was a pistol in the glove box of the truck, and all I could think about was coming in here and shooting that bastard's dick off."

"I'm so sorry he did this to you."

"I'm so sorry I missed. I meant to kill him. Maim him first. Then kill him."

Lorna leaned closer. "Maybe tell the police it was self-defense."

The next day, the whole family was together at the ranch. Duke insisted they all be under one roof so he could feed and hug them throughout the day, and Mack couldn't argue with his logic.

He and Lorna hadn't had much of a chance to talk, but he hadn't let her or the kids out of his sight all day.

It had been a long night. Elizabeth had shown up, and she and Ford had driven Mack and Lorna to the emergency room. He'd been checked out, cleared of a concussion, and the doctor had stitched up the cut on his head from the coffee cup Lyle had hit him with.

Lorna had also been cleared of a concussion, but it hurt his heart every time he looked at the purple and black bruises Lyle's fist had left around her eye and the small steri-strips holding the cut on her brow together.

Knox had come to the hospital, and it was past three in the morning by the time they'd given their statements and been released.

The pain meds had made Lorna drowsy, and she'd fallen asleep in the truck, so Ford had driven them both back to the ranch, and Dodge promised he and Maisie would bring the kids out first thing in the morning.

For all they'd been through, he was thankful they'd escaped with only bruises and a few stitches.

Misty hadn't been as lucky. She'd been admitted to the hospital, and they'd had another chance to talk to her before they left. She told them that along with multiple contusions, she was dehydrated, her arm was fractured in two places, she had a couple of broken ribs, and a ruptured spleen.

Apparently, Lyle had beaten her then kept her locked in the bedroom of her trailer for the last several days. She said he told her he was coming into some big money and then they were going to Florida. Together. He'd locked her in the room when she'd told him she wasn't going anywhere with him, except to hell.

Which was apparently going to have to wait for Lyle Williams.

The gun shot ripped through his chest, but unfortunately, missed any vital organs. Which had the fortunate effect of saving Misty from going to prison and instead would send Lyle there for breaking and entering, domestic violence, and attempted manslaughter, just for starters.

Chevy and Leni had arrived home midmorning and couldn't believe everything that had gone on while they were away. Chevy swore he was never leaving Colorado again, and Leni and Lorna disappeared into Ford's bedroom for a few hours, the two sisters needing time together to talk through all that had happened.

Judy Fitzgerald stopped by after lunch and had asked to speak to them, and Mack took Lorna's hand as the three of them stepped out onto the porch.

Lorna could barely meet the other woman's eyes. "I'm so ashamed of the way Lyle treated you, Judy. And that you saw him treating me that way."

"You have nothing to be ashamed of," Judy told her. "And don't you dare apologize for that ass-wipe. I've known men like him before, and I knew something wasn't right the minute you walked into my office."

"So, did you come out here to tell us that the paperwork went through?" Lorna asked. "Does the shop belong to Lyle now?"

Judy huffed and shook her head. "No, I came to give you this." She handed Lorna the paperwork that she and Lyle had signed. "If either of you would have looked closer at the document, you would have seen that although this form does say 'transfer of ownership' on it, it's used to transfer ownership of assets from a deceased person to their heirs. It was the only one I could think of that looked similar to the real business one and had a place to fill in an address. I thought that would make it seem more legit. But Lyle actually signed his name on the line for the deceased."

Lorna gaped at her. "Are you serious?"

"Yes, I am. And even if I *had* used the right form, it would absolutely have had to have been signed in front of a notary. And I don't care what Lyle says, it's against the law for a notary to stamp their seal if they didn't actually witness and record the signatures."

"I knew that wasn't how it was done."

"So, what does this mean?" Mack asked. "Did you still request the deed to be sent up here from Denver?"

"Oh no. I made all that up, too. The deed for the building is in a file in my office. I just knew something Lyle was pulling something shady, and I was trying to buy you some extra time."

Lorna threw her arms around the woman. "Thank you so much."

Judy hugged her back. "Don't you worry. The building is still in your name, the coffee shop is still your business, and as far as the clerk and recorder's office is concerned, this whole thing was just one big clerical error that is now corrected and will soon be forgotten."

Mack gave her a hug too. "You are one crafty clerk."

Judy shrugged. "I know." She squeezed Lorna's hand. "You take care of yourself. You've got a good man now. Don't let the fear of the past stand in the way of your present happiness."

Lorna nodded. "Thank you."

Judy waved as she headed back to her car. "See you

next week, Mack, for Dylan's next horseback riding lessons."

"You bet," Mack called back. "As many as he wants."

Lorna slumped against him as Judy drove away. "I can't believe it. When I saw her at the door, I was sure she was here to tell me my business was gone."

"She's one clever lady," Mack told her. "She gave me some pretty good advice the other day, too. She said if you find your person, the one who makes you happy, and who you can't imagine living your life without, they're worth doing the work to have a relationship with."

"Yeah, so that's kind of what I wanted to talk to you about today," Lorna said, taking a seat on the porch steps and patting the spot beside her.

His heart filled with dread as he sat down next to her.

He'd been here before.

This was the part where she'd say he wasn't worth it, that she and the kids didn't want him in their lives anymore.

Lorna turned her body toward his. "I wanted to tell you that I'm not interested in pretending to be a couple anymore."

He knew it.

"Okay, I understand," he said with a resigned sigh. "But before you go, I just want you to know that even though we were faking the whole couple thing, the feelings were all real to me."

"You don't understand—," she tried to say, but he cut her off.

"Please, let me get this out, then you can go, and I'll never say another word about it. But I have to tell you that I am in love with you, Lorna Gibbs. And I'm in love with Max and Izzy, and even that scruffy dog, too. I know we haven't been together for very long, but I fell for you the first day we met. I thought you were so great those first few months we were hanging out together. And when we were apart, I thought about you every day. Since I've been back, and we've been spending time together, I've fallen even harder. I understand this is a lot for you, and that you told me you just wanted to be friends, and I didn't honor that. But I swear, I'll try to abide by it now, because I can't imagine not having you and the kids in my life. Even if it's just as friends."

"You didn't let me finish. And you're the one who doesn't understand. I'm trying to tell you that I don't want to be a pretend couple anymore…because I want us to be the real thing."

He blinked at her, afraid to believe what he was hearing. "You do?"

"Yes, I do. I'm in love with you, too. I've been trying to fight it, trying to protect my heart because I couldn't bear to have you break it and to have another man leave me and my kids. But I couldn't do it. Time and time again, you've been there for me, for us. It's not easy taking on a single mom with two kids, and most men wouldn't want to. But you've shown me how much you care, not just about me, but about Max and Izzy, and I'm putting my trust in you that you want leave or hurt us."

"I won't ever leave you," he said, still dazed from hearing she was in love with him too. "I know what it's like to be left behind, and I'm not that guy. I'm the one who stays. I'm here for you, and I'll always help you with whatever you need."

"I just need *you*. I love the way you are always willing to help me, and everyone else—."

"Being useful is what makes people want to keep me around."

"That's not true. Your willingness to help is a wonderful quality about you, and the way you anticipate my needs makes me feel cherished and cared for, but that's not the only thing I love about you. You are kind and thoughtful, and you make me laugh. You care about me and my kids, and you don't just tell us, you *show* us by listening and being there. I don't want you because you help me clean the kitchen, although I don't want you to stop doing that—it's sexy as hell when you load the dishwasher—or because you're willing to clean my gutters or mow my lawn. I can hire a handyman for that. I want you for you."

He ducked his head, not used to hearing this kind of praise. But her words meant everything to him. "Thank you. That means a lot. But I'm still going to clean the gutters and mow the lawn."

"As long as you do it with your shirt off…"

They laughed together, then she reached up and laid a hand on his cheek. "I know this isn't gonna be easy or perfect right away. I'm terrible at folding the laundry, and Leni says I occasionally snore. I make great spaghetti, but we tend to rotate the same five meals every week, and I'm ridiculous about clipping coupons. I hate sharing popcorn at the movies, and Max can have a total meltdown if he gets too tired. So, we still have plenty of things to figure out."

A grin tugged at his lips. "Something I learned from playing checkers with your son is that when it's your game, you can make up the rules, and we can play it however we want."

She grinned back. "He is a pretty smart kid."

He picked up her hand then drew in a breath and released it. "I've spent my whole life wishing for a real family. Growing up, I always felt lost. Like I was always the one on the inside looking in. The lost kid who no one ever bothered to find. Then last year, I learned I had three brothers and a grandfather who lived on a ranch in Colorado. I came out here hoping to find a family, but I never imagined that I'd find a home. And that's what I feel when I'm with you and Max and Izzy. That I'm finally home."

"I love you, Mack Lassiter. You're not a lost cowboy anymore. We found you, and we're not letting you go." Lorna climbed into his lap, put her arms around him and pressed a hard kiss to his lips. "You're stuck with us now, a rambunctious six-year-old, an adorable infant, a scruffy dog that might possibly have fleas, a baby cow named Kevin, and a hot mess of a single mom."

"Sound perfect to me. And I told you before, darlin'," he said, laughing as he nuzzled her neck. "Hot messes are my favorite kind."

The end…
…and just the beginning.

If you or someone you know is experiencing abuse in a relationship and needs help...

National Domestic Violence Hot Line
Call 1-800-799-SAFE (7233)
Or
Text "START" (88788)
For Free Confidential Help

I hope you loved Mack and Lorna's story! If you did, please consider leaving a review.★

And if you haven't fallen in love with all the cowboys of Lassiter Ranch yet…

Find the whole series on Amazon.

Save the Date for a Cowboy:
Prequel Novella to the Lassiter Ranch series
Love at First Cowboy:
Book 1
Overdue for a Cowboy:
Book 2
Second Chance with a Cowboy:
Book 3

Thanks for reading—I write these stories for you!

Be the first to find out when my next books are releasing and hear all the latest news and updates happening by signing up for the Jennie Marts newsletter at: Jenniemarts.com

My biggest thanks goes out to my readers! Thank you for loving my stories and my characters. I would love to invite you to join my street team, Jennie's Page Turners!

If you want MORE hot cowboys, meet three brothers who are hockey-playing cowboys in the
Cowboys of Creedence series:
Caught Up in a Cowboy
You Had Me at Cowboy
It Started with a Cowboy
Wish Upon a Cowboy

Even more hunky cowboys can be found in the heartwarming (but still steamy)
Creedence Horse Rescue series:
A Cowboy State of Mind
When a Cowboy Loves a Woman
How to Cowboy
Never Enough Cowboy
Every Bit a Cowboy
A Cowboy Country Christmas

If you enjoy small town contemporary romance with cute cowboys-
Try the **Hearts of Montana series:**
Tucked Away
Hidden Away
Stolen Away

If you like hockey romance with cute hockey players and steamy romance-
Try the **Bannister Brothers Books**:
Icing on the Date
Skirting the Ice
Worth the Shot

More small-town romantic comedy can be found in the -
Cotton Creek Romance series:
Romancing the Ranger
Hooked On Love
Catching the Cowgirl

If you love mysteries with humor and romance, be sure to check out **The Page Turners Series** where a group of women in a book club search for clues and romance while eating really great desserts.

Another Saturday Night and I Ain't Got No Body
Easy Like Sunday Mourning
Just Another Maniac Monday
Tangled Up In Tuesday
What To Do About Wednesday
A Halloween Hookup: A Holiday Novella
A Cowboy for Christmas: A Holiday Novella

Even more humor-filled mystery fun can be found in my new **Bee Keeping cozy mystery series**:
Take the Honey and Run
Kill or Bee Killed

Thanks for reading and loving my books!

ABOUT THE AUTHOR

Jennie Marts is the *USA TODAY* Best-selling author of award-winning books filled with love, laughter, and always a happily ever after. Readers call her books "laugh out loud" funny and the "perfect mix of romance, humor, and steam." Fic Central claimed one of her books was "the most fun I've had reading in years."

She is living her own happily ever after in the mountains of Colorado with her husband, two dogs, and a parakeet who loves to tweet to the oldies. She's addicted to Diet Coke, adores Cheetos, and believes you can't have too many books, shoes, or friends.

Her books range from western romance to cozy mysteries, but they all have the charm and appeal of quirky small-town life. She loves genre-mashups like adding romance to her Page Turners cozy mysteries and creating the hockey-playing cowboys in the Cowboys of Creedence. The same small-town community comes to life with more animal antics in her latest Creedence Horse Rescue series. And Take the Honey and Run and **Kill or Bee Killed** are the newest cozy mysteries in the **Bee Keeping Mystery** series.

Jennie loves to hear from readers. Follow her on Facebook at Jennie Marts Books, Twitter at @JennieMarts, and at jenniemartswriter on Instagram. Visit her at www.jenniemarts.com and sign up for her newsletter to keep up with the latest news and releases.

Printed in Great Britain
by Amazon